Famous Mistakes

Read all the mysteries in the

NANCY DREW DIARIES

Nancy Drew DIARIES™

Famous Mistakes

#17

CAROLYN KEENE

Aladdin
NEW YORK LONDON TORONTO SYDNEY NEW DELHI

ALADDIN

An imprint of Simon & Schuster Children's Publishing Division

1230 Avenue of the Americas, New York, New York 10020

First Aladdin hardcover edition January 2019

Text copyright © 2019 by Simon & Schuster, Inc.

Jacket illustration copyright © 2019 by Erin McGuire

Also available in an Aladdin paperback edition.

For information about special discounts for bulk purchases, please contact Simon & Schuster Special Sales at 1-866-506-1949 or business@simonandschuster.com.

The Simon & Schuster Speakers Bureau can bring authors to your live event. For more information or to book an event contact the Simon & Schuster Speakers Bureau at 1-866-248-3049 or visit our website at www.simonspeakers.com.

Series designed by Karin Paprocki

Jacket designed by Nina Simoneaux

Interior designed by Mike Rosamilia

The text of this book was set in Adobe Caslon Pro.

Manufactured in the United States of America 1218 FFG

2 4 6 8 10 9 7 5 3 1

Library of Congress Cataloging-in-Publication Data

Names: Keene, Carolyn, author.

Title: Famous mistakes / by Carolyn Keene.

Description: First Aladdin hardcover/paperback edition. | New York : Aladdin, 2018. | Series: Nancy Drew diaries ; #17 | Summary: Nancy and her sleuthing friends race to find out who is responsible for sabotaging a controversial comedian's upcoming performance at River Heights's new arts complex, where an exhibition of Dutch Masters is being installed.

Identifiers: LCCN 2017058788 (print) | LCCN 2018004182 (eBook) | ISBN 9781481485517 (eBook) | ISBN 9781481485494 (pbk) | ISBN 9781481485500 (hc)

Subjects: | CYAC: Mystery and detective stories. | Comedians—Fiction. | Sabotage—Fiction.

Classification: LCC PZ7.K23 (eBook) | LCC PZ7.K23 Fb 2018 (print) | DDC [Fic]—dc23

LC record available at https://lccn.loc.gov/2017058788

Contents

Dear Diary,

YOU NEVER KNOW WHEN A CASE IS GOING to hit. The other day I thought I was just going to help Ned interview famous stand-up comedian Brady Owens for his podcast, but instead I found myself investigating who was trying to sabotage him. To say this case turned out different than I expected is the understatement of the year. It was a doozy!

CHAPTER ONE

Great Expectations

"HERE, LET ME TAKE ONE OF THOSE FOR you," I said to my boyfriend, Ned, as I watched him struggle to carry two boxes of recording gear.

"That would be great." Ned said. "Thanks, Nancy."

"No problem," I said. "After all, we can't have you getting sweaty before your big interview." Ned was interviewing Brady Owens, a famous stand-up comedian, for his podcast, NED Talks. He'd been so anxious about getting to the hotel on time that we ended up half an hour early, so we'd been walking laps around the block to help him work off some of his nervous energy. Ned and I have been a couple for a few years and we've known each other since we were little kids, but I had never seen him like this. I mean, he'd barely touched his breakfast—usually he's a bottomless pit and can eat endless amounts of food—but I'd caught his hands shaking as he tried to drink his juice.

"Thanks," Ned said as he handed me one of the boxes. "It was really nice of George to lend me all this stuff. It's really going to make NED Talks sound a lot more professional."

George is one of my best friends. She has the latest gadgets, and we sometimes joke that she's part robot because she seems to have an innate sense of how machines work. We may tease her now and then, but I was always really grateful for her tech savvy. A lot of cases would have gone unsolved without her help.

"I just wish she'd been able to switch her shift at the Coffee Cabin so she could come with you. I don't think I'm going to be much help," I said, looking down at the box I was carrying.

"Don't worry. George was very thorough in

explaining how to set everything up. And who could be more of a help than a world-famous detective?" Ned said with a grin.

I laughed. "I'm not world-famous!"

I am an amateur sleuth, and I've helped people with stuff like stolen items or blackmail attempts. People find a teenage girl detective memorable, so I am known around River Heights area but I'm hardly world-famous.

"Oh, really?" Ned asked, raising an eyebrow. "Because just yesterday, when I was at Morwin's Bagel Shoppe, the guy behind the counter asked if I knew the local teen sleuth."

Ned has always been one of my biggest fans. He's helped me solve a ton of cases. I was glad to return the favor and be able to help him with one of his passions. I may not know how the equipment works, but I do know how to carry a box.

"Seriously," Ned continued. "I'm really glad you're here. This is a big deal for me, and I feel a lot calmer with you around."

I shifted the box I was carrying and squeezed his shoulder reassuringly. "You're going to do great."

"Thanks," he said. "It's just that Brady Owens is the most controversial comedian in the country right now. This interview is big, and I really don't want to make a fool of myself."

I completely understood why Ned was feeling nervous. He had started his NED Talks podcast just over a year ago. He interviewed musicians, actors, and other artists on his college campus. He had a loyal fan base, mostly fellow students at his school, but Brady Owens was on a completely different level than the sophomore singer-songwriter who performed every week at the student center. "I also really don't want to let your dad down," Ned said. "He went out on a limb to help me get this interview." Brady and my dad had been in the same fraternity in college—Brady was actually discovered at an open mic hosted by their fraternity—so when Ned read that Brady was coming back to River Heights to perform at the recently opened Arts Complex, Ned screwed up his courage to ask my dad for an introduction to Brady.

"Don't worry about my dad," I said. "Just focus on what you need to do to feel ready for the interview."

We rounded the corner and stood in front of the Towering Heights Resort, the fanciest hotel in town. I checked the time. We were still ten minutes early.

"Do you want to do another lap around the block?" I asked.

"Let's watch the video again," Ned said.

"Are you sure? You've watched it at least one hundred times. And it happened only two weeks ago!"

Ned nodded. "I'm his first interview since it happened. I need to make sure all my facts are straight when I ask him about it."

"Okay," I said, pointing toward a bench nearby. "Let's go over there." We sat down and I pulled out my phone and typed in *Brady Owens Heckler*. The first result was the video we were looking for. It had over ten million views.

Brady stood onstage in a comedy club, microphone in his hand, pacing in front of a stool.

"So, last night I was walking home after hanging out with some friends. It was late, and I turn the corner on this deserted street, and I see this guy mugging this old lady. He's trying to grab her purse, so I run over to help."

He holds a beat.

"Eventually, we got it off her."

The audience breaks into laughter. Brady waits for it to die down and then continues. "Mugging jokes—always funny. I think it's the word 'mugging'—"

Before he can get further, a woman from the audience yells, "Actually, violence is never funny!"

Boos echo throughout the audience, and Brady whips toward her. The expression on his face is livid.

"You know what's never funny," he hisses. "Interrupting." He lifts his head up, addressing the whole crowd. "You know what we should do? We should mug this woman in the parking lot. That'll teach her not to interrupt. Plus, it will be funny."

There is some laughter and applause in the audience, but there are also gasps and a smattering of boos.

The video cut off there, but the reaction was immediate once the video was posted online. People were furious at Brady. They thought he had crossed the line and encouraged violence against the heckler, but Brady was unapologetic. In a series of tweets the next day, he said everyone was being too sensitive. He argued that it was clear he was joking. Besides, stand-up comedians were supposed to offend people.

I thought his reaction to the heckler had been way out of line and really dangerous. At the very least, that woman deserved a sincere apology. I knew Ned was planning on pushing Brady on the subject, and I was looking forward to hearing what Brady would say.

"I can't believe I landed this first interview. I'm just an amateur podcaster!"

"All 'amateur' means is that you don't get paid. It doesn't mean you don't know what you're doing."

Ned smiled at me. "Thanks, Nancy."

I checked my watch again. It was time to go.

"You ready?" I asked Ned.

Ned nodded.

We both stopped short when we entered the hotel lobby. They had completely renovated since the last time we had been in.

"Wow," Ned said. "They really made this place look beautiful."

"Yeah," I agreed. The old lobby had been nice, but this was gorgeous. Crystal chandeliers hung from an impossibly high ceiling. The dark mahogany pillars lining the room played off the mahogany welcome counter and tables throughout, along with maroon velvet chairs that were scattered about invitingly. To top it off, a man in a tuxedo played a grand piano in the center of the space.

"I knew they were renovating, but I had no idea it was going to be like this," Ned said.

"They must really believe the new Arts Complex is going to bring more tourists to River Heights," I said. The Arts Complex had been the passion project of the River Heights mayor, and it had just opened last month. It had a theater, where Brady Owens would be performing tonight, that could be used to show movies, plays, or other performances; an art museum, which promised to feature a wide variety of works; and a full set of classrooms and practice spaces that people could rent. They were offering classes in both the actual craft of art, like drawing and painting, and art history. These were the types of classes you would usually find on a university campus, but they were all open to the public.

Ned checked his phone. "Brady said he's in room 823."

"It looks like the elevators are in that corner," I said, pointing to the back left.

We rode up in silence. I could tell that Ned was running through his questions in his head, and I didn't want to bother him.

We arrived on the eighth floor and stepped off the elevator.

"Eight twenty-three is all the way at the end," I said, reading the signs.

Ned nodded and we headed down the long hallway. The carpet was plush beneath our feet.

We arrived at the room, and Ned took a deep breath before knocking on the door. "Here goes nothing."

As soon as his knuckles made contact, the door started to swing open.

"That's weird," Ned said.

"Maybe he forgot to close the door all the way," I suggested.

Ned nudged the door open a touch more. "Hello?" he called out. "Mr. Owens? Are you there? It's Ned Nickerson and Nancy Drew from the NED Talks podcast."

There was no response.

I moved in front of him and knocked on the door loudly. "Mr. Owens?" I yelled. There was still no response.

I gently pushed the door open, revealing the entire room.

"Oh my gosh," Ned and I said in unison. The room was a mess. It had been completely trashed. Brady's suitcase had been opened and his clothing was strewn around the entire room. The sheets had been stripped off the bed. The lamps were on the floor, the light-bulbs shattered. Even the paintings had been taken off the wall. I've seen a lot of rooms destroyed, but this was one of the most drastically defaced rooms I had ever seen. Not to mention that one very important thing was missing.

"Where's Brady?" Ned asked.

CHAPTER TWO

False Alarm

"I'M GOING TO CALL HIM," NED SAID.

"Good idea," I said as I put down the box of equipment and stepped into the room to get a better look, my detective Spidey-sense taking over. I might not officially be on a case, but this trashed room was definitely a mystery. Something had happened in this room, and I felt compelled to find out as much about it as I could. I carefully stepped over the scattered clothing, broken glass, and ripped paper, not wanting to disturb anything in case the police came to investigate later. A laptop was poking out from underneath a sweater. Brady was on a twelve-city tour. His laptop was likely one of the most valuable items he had with him while he was traveling. If the culprit hadn't taken that, this wouldn't be a random theft. It wasn't just someone looking for valuables. At the same time, I didn't see a note. If it was a saboteur, they would want their victim to know why they'd been targeted. In other words, I had no idea what had happened here.

"He's not answering," Ned called from the hallway. "I'm really getting worried. You don't think he was kidnapped, do you?"

I studied the room. I felt my stomach sink as I realized that this mess definitely could have been caused by a struggle.

"I don't know," I said to Ned. "Let's go down to the front desk and notify security. They probably have security cameras that caught what happened."

"Let's go," Ned said, charging back toward the elevators.

I hurried after him, grabbing my box of equipment

on the way. Ned was standing at the elevator, pushing the down button over and over again.

"I don't think pushing the button more makes the elevator come any faster," I teased.

Ned gave me a wry smile. "I know. Sorry. I'm just really freaked out."

"I get it," I said. "Don't worry, though. We'll figure this out."

The elevator arrived and Ned and I hopped on. As soon as the doors opened at the lobby, we raced toward the front desk.

"Nancy Drew? Is that you?" the clerk asked. I immediately recognized the freckled face waving at me.

"Pete DeHaro!" I exclaimed.

"Yeah, it's me!" said Pete.

"How's Jake?" I asked.

Pete lit up. "He's great! We just got him a new chew toy that he loves. He carries it with him all over the house." Jake was Pete's beloved German shepherd–golden retriever mix. I had helped Pete track him down a little over a year ago. It was no simple missing-dog case, though—we'd ended up uncovering a ring of dog thieves!

"I still owe you one, Nancy. You totally saved Jake," Pete told me.

"Thanks, Pete," I said. "But it was no trouble. I was happy to help!"

I felt Ned nudge me. We didn't have any time to waste.

"What's going on?" Pete asked. He leaned in to whisper. "Is there a case going on at the hotel?"

"Maybe," I said. I explained how we had found Brady's room and that we were concerned for the comedian's safety. "Do you think we could check the security cameras?" I asked.

Pete grimaced. "Well, as part of the renovation, they actually got rid of the cameras in the hallways," he said. "We only have them in the lobby now."

"Why?" I asked. That seemed odd.

Pete shrugged. "They did a survey, and guests said they valued privacy over every other category. I guess they figured cameras in the lobby were enough."

I paused for a moment, feeling stymied on how to move forward at this point. It felt premature to call the police, but I wasn't sure what else to do.

"Did you say it was room 823?" asked Pete. "The guest, Brady Owens, he's that comedian who yelled at the heckler, right?"

"Yeah, that's him," Ned said.

"I think I saw him going into our restaurant a little while ago," Pete said.

"Really?" Ned asked.

"Yeah," Pete said. "It's right down that hallway."

"Thanks, Pete!" I said, turning to go. "Give Jake a pat on the head for me."

"Will do," Pete said to our backs as Ned and I hurried toward the restaurant.

Like the rest of the hotel, the restaurant had changed a lot since the last time I had been there. Instead of the geometric-patterned carpet and pink vinyl booths, they had completely altered the look. It now had dark floors and dark walls with exposed beams in the ceiling. In the corner was another piano, providing the restaurant with its own music. It was the kind of place where you could imagine people having a romantic dinner or closing a business deal.

"Over there," Ned said, pointing to a table in the back corner. Brady was sitting with another man around the same age. It was odd to see Brady in person after watching his video online so many times with Ned. He wore black jeans, a black sweater, and chunky glasses, just as he had in the video, but he looked smaller, more delicate in real life. In the video, under the lights and being so angry, he'd seemed intimidating, but sitting there in the restaurant, he seemed almost vulnerable. I wondered if he'd been a kid who had been bullied a lot and who had learned how to be quick-witted and funny as a defense mechanism.

Ned led the way to the table.

"Mr. Owens?" he asked, his voice a little too loud for the environment. A number of heads turned in our direction.

Brady's head shot up, his eyes wide. He looked genuinely afraid, as if he was worried that Ned might accost him. Ned noticed too. He took a deep breath and spoke more slowly and calmly.

"I'm Ned Nickerson. We had an interview scheduled for my podcast—"

"NED Talks!" Brady yelped. Now he was the one speaking a little too loudly. He looked at his phone. "I am so sorry! I didn't hear my phone ring over the music. I lost track of time, getting caught up with Joe Archer here." He indicated the man sitting across from him. "Do you know Joe Archer?" he asked, finally taking a breath.

Ned shook his head. "Not personally," he said. "Of course, I know who you are." I did too. Joe Archer was the director of the new Arts Complex. There had been a lot of articles about him since the complex opened last month. He was a River Heights native who had gone to college here. He had spent the last several years managing a famous arts space in San Francisco, and it was considered a huge deal that he had come back to River Heights to manage our Arts Complex. The town had high hopes that the connections he had built in San Francisco would allow him to bring world-class talent to River Heights.

"But—" Ned tried to continue, but Brady just spoke over him.

"Joe, this is Ned Nickerson, and this is . . ." He turned to me. "And who is this young lady?"

"I'm Nancy Drew," I said.

"Nancy Drew!" Brady exclaimed. "Dare I ask if you are Carson Drew's daughter?"

"I am," I confirmed.

"Joe was in the same fraternity with Carson and me," he explained. "How is Carson? We invited him to join us, but he said he had a brief due to a judge."

"He's well," I said. "But, yes, busy. I know he's looking forward to your show, though."

"Here, here. Have a seat. We can order you some sodas while Joe and I finish eating and then we can do the interview."

"That's a really nice offer," I said, "but I'm afraid we have some bad news."

"Bad news?" Brady asked. "What are you talking about?"

"We went up to your room before we found you here. . . ." Ned faltered. I could tell he wasn't sure how exactly to break it to him.

"The room was destroyed," I said, bailing Ned out.

"What?" said Brady, confused.

"It looked like someone had gone through all your stuff. Your clothes were everywhere. The art was off the wall."

Brady looked back and forth between us. I could see him processing what we had just told him.

"That's outrageous. How would anyone even know where you're staying?" Joe asked.

Brady sighed. "Probably has something to do with my tweet this morning. Thought I was giving this hotel some good publicity."

Brady pulled out his phone to show us a photo of him opening his hotel room door to reveal the fancy room. He captioned it, "Just checked into the amazing Towering Heights Resort for my show tonight!"

His hotel room number was clearly visible over his shoulder.

"Brady!" Joe admonished. "You'll have to change rooms; we have to call the police."

Brady shook his head. "No, not yet. I want to see it." He turned to me. "This is very important. Did you see if there was a little black leather notebook with an elastic band around it in there?"

I thought back to the room, trying to remember if I had seen the notebook, but it didn't come to mind.

"I don't know . . . I'm sorry. I saw your laptop. They didn't take that."

Brady stood up, almost knocking his chair down in the process. He threw his napkin on the table.

"I don't care about the laptop. I only care about the notebook."

He raced toward the door. Not knowing what else to do, Ned, Joe Archer, and I all followed behind him. Brady passed a waitress.

"Your bill, Mr. Owens?" she asked.

Brady stopped, pulled out his wallet, and handed

her two twenty-dollar bills. "Just charge the meal to room 823. These are for you. Thanks for everything," he said, not giving her a chance to respond.

Brady picked up the pace, so that he was moving at closer to a jog than a walk. As we made our way through the lobby, slaloming through the overstuffed chairs and dodging rolling suitcases, I could feel the eyes of all the guests on us. I couldn't blame them. From the outside, we probably looked ridiculous. Two grown men, Ned, and me sprinting through the elevator lobby, Ned and I still lugging our boxes of recording equipment.

We got to the elevator and Brady was finally forced to stop. He hit the button over and over again, just like Ned had a few minutes earlier.

"What's so important about the notebook?" I asked.

Brady paced back and forth. He was so distracted he hadn't heard me.

"What's so important about the notebook?" I repeated. Brady turned and looked at me. I saw the same flash of anger I had seen right before he'd cut into the heckler. I physically took a step back, wanting to put a little more space between us. I realized that Brady was the type of person whose emotions could turn on a dime.

"Oh, nothing," he snapped. "Just all the material I've spent the past year writing." He looked at us, waiting a beat for dramatic effect. Even in a moment of crisis, he maintained his performer instinct. "So, you know, just my entire life!"

CHAPTER THREE

A Girl on a Mission

BRADY HIT THE ELEVATOR BUTTON AGAIN. The number display showed that it was stopped on the fourth floor.

"Forget it," Brady said, exasperated. "I'm taking the stairs."

"You're on the eighth floor," Joe Archer protested.

"Nothing wrong with a little exercise," said Brady, already heading toward the stairs. Like ducklings following their mother, we trailed after him.

We raced down a hallway, past a shelf of brochures and a bulletin board of posters advertising local activities. Something caught my attention out of the corner of my eye, but we were moving too fast for me to make it out. I slowed down to get a better look. When I was a less experienced detective, I wouldn't have bothered. I would have thought keeping up with Brady was the most important thing I could do, but over the years I had learned that trusting your gut can sometimes be the key to solving a case. Those "flashes" when something seems out of place can be your brain realizing something, but not processing it fast enough for it to make sense to you.

"What's up, Nancy?" Ned asked.

"I'm not sure," I said scanning the board. "I saw something that I think might be important." I spotted a poster for an exhibit of paintings from the Dutch Golden Age that would be opening at the Arts Complex soon. That wasn't what I had noticed, but I snapped a photo on my phone for Bess. She's my other best friend and George-the-tech-genius's cousin. She's not really into technology but is a huge fan of the Dutch masters. Especially Rembrandt. I knew one of her dreams was to go to the Netherlands to visit the Rijksmuseum, which has the largest collection of Dutch Golden Age paintings in the world. I couldn't wait to tell her that some of these paintings would be coming right to River Heights. She would be beyond excited.

I went back to searching the board. Suddenly I saw it. It was a poster for Brady's show, but across his picture the word *BOYCOTT* was scrawled. Underneath that were the letters *RHVRA*, almost like a signature.

"There," I said, pointing at the poster. Ned came over to get a look.

"What does 'RHVRA' mean?" he asked.

"*RH* probably stands for River Heights, but I don't know about the rest of it," I said. "But if someone is mad enough to organize a boycott and vandalize a poster, they might be mad enough to trash Brady's room."

"This is definitely a clue," Ned said.

I agreed. I heard a door shut and realized that Brady and Joe had reached the stairs while we had been lingering at the bulletin board.

"We should catch up," I said, pulling the poster off

the board. "We'll show this to Brady and Joe. They might know what 'RHVRA' stands for."

Ned and I rushed to the doorway we had seen Joe and Brady go through and started climbing the stairs to Brady's floor. We could hear footsteps echoing down as the two men climbed above us. We were winded and sweaty by the time we reached Brady's room. My arms felt like jelly from lugging the box of recording equipment all over the hotel.

Brady and Joe were already in the room and the door was slightly ajar when we got there. I slowly pushed it open. Brady was sitting on the bed, his shoulders slumped, his head down. Joe was standing above him, his hand on his friend's shoulder, trying to comfort him.

Ned and I exchanged a look. This was not good.

"The notebook is gone?" I asked, stepping farther into the room.

"I wish," Brady said. I looked at him, confused. Why would he wish it was gone? Before I could ask, he continued, "If it were gone, I could get it back." He lifted up his hands, showing us shredded-up pieces of notebook paper, scraps of writing visible. "The monsters destroyed it."

"I am so sorry," I said.

"I spent a year working on that material. I'm supposed to perform it for the first time on the Comedy Channel in a month. It was going to be my big break."

"Do you remember any of it?" asked Ned.

Brady snapped his head toward Ned, sparks of anger flying behind his eyes. "Sure, I remember the gist of it, but people think comedy is *so* easy. You just go up there, you tell a few jokes, and the people laugh."

"I don't think it's easy," Ned tried to interject, but Brady was off on a tirade. I was starting to realize that this was a pattern with him.

"But it's a lot more complicated than that. Comedy is about precision. You need exactly the right words in exactly the right order. Every pause in my routine, every 'and' instead of 'but,' it's all labored over. Because here's a secret: audiences—they don't want to see you succeed. They want to see you fail. Your job is to win them over, and winning them over requires perfection. So now, thanks to whoever did this, I'm going to bomb on national television and my career is going to be over."

Brady took a deep breath, running his hands through his hair. I decided to take advantage of this brief pause and jump in. Who knew when my next opportunity would be, at the rate Brady spoke?

"I found something that might tell us who did it," I said.

"We all know who did it!" Brady shouted.

"We do?" I asked.

"The same people who have been attacking me online for one dumb joke I made. Now they're moving their harassment to real life. They think that if they throw me off my game by trashing my room, by destroying my notebook, I'll bomb tonight."

"But if they're boycotting you, why do they care how well you do?"

"It's a lot easier to convince people to boycott a bad show," Brady explained. "If I did amazing tonight and everyone who's in the audience goes online and tells all their friends and followers that Brady Owens's show was awesome, then people who live in Amherst, Massachusetts, the next stop on my tour, are going to have to really be convinced that what I said was so terrible that they shouldn't go. But if they hear that I was horrible and not funny at all, then it's really easy for them to say, 'Yeah, he is a terrible person. I'm not going to support him.'"

"That feels like you're oversimplifying," I said.

"Oh, you want nuance?" Brady asked. "These little jerks found my home address and they faked 911 calls coming from there. The police literally surrounded my house."

Vandalizing the poster seemed a lot more harmless than destroying his room or spoofing his number to call the police.

"I found this poster downstairs," I said, and showed it to the others. Brady and Joe leaned in for a closer look.

"Oh, dear," Joe sighed. "Yep. They probably are involved."

"What is RHVRA?" Brady asked.

"River Heights Victims' Rights Advocates," Joe said. "They have been calling and e-mailing my office constantly, imploring me to cancel your show because you don't respect crime victims. There's even a group of them sitting in the waiting area of my office as we speak, demanding to speak to me."

"Wow. Well, thanks for not canceling," Brady said.

"Look, I don't necessarily agree with your decision to put that heckler on the spot like that, but I would never cancel your show over it," Joe said. "I don't cancel a show just because I, or a community, disagree with it. Freedom of expression—the First Amendment—is a fundamental American principle, and I believe that it is especially important for the arts. Bottom line, it's going to take more than some angry protesters sitting in my office to get me to cancel a show. To my mind, that just means that it's even more important to let the show go on."

I thought about what Joe was saying. Brady had— jokingly or not—encouraged violence against someone.

That was going beyond just voicing a different opinion. I wasn't sure Brady or Joe was completely in the right on this.

"Why didn't you apologize?" I asked. "If not for the joke, then for telling the crowd to mug the woman who shouted at you?"

Brady sighed and ran his hand through his hair. "I didn't realize it was going to turn into this whole thing. In the moment, it didn't feel like a big deal. I have to shut down hecklers in my show all the time. It's just a fact of being a comic. It wasn't until the next morning that I realized it had spun out of control."

"Okay . . . ," I said, not seeing why this meant he couldn't apologize.

"By the time I saw how badly people had reacted, it had turned into a mob. My Twitter was filled with people calling me the most vile names. Ironically, given how this all started, plenty of them were calling for violence against me. And I'm not going to reward that behavior. They don't get to do these horrible things and win."

"We'll get you more security," Joe said.

"No," said Brady sharply. "I don't want that."

"I'm afraid it wasn't a suggestion. If you want this show to go on, we're going to need to bring in some extra security to make sure the event is safe for all our guests. We don't know what these people have planned next."

"No. If they see that I'm easily intimidated, they'll just grow bolder and bolder each stop on my tour."

"Well, no offense to the people of Amherst and wherever you go after that, but my priority is the safety of the people of River Heights. You are one of the first shows at our venue, and I can't have anything go wrong or we could risk the complex's entire future."

Brady puffed up his shoulders and moved right into Joe's space. Joe was a good six inches taller than the comedian, but Brady still managed to seem threatening.

"This is so typical of you, Joe. You always prioritize your own needs over everybody else's. . . ."

"Oh, really?" Joe asked, leaning down so he was just inches from Brady's face.

Ned and I exchanged looks. This was quickly escalating into a personal fight that seemed to have roots way back in their history.

"What if I found the culprit?" I asked. Joe and Brady slowly pivoted to look at me, but they didn't say anything. "Listen, I think this is the work of one person. It sounds like RHVRA is a group of concerned citizens that want to talk to you, Joe. They've been waiting in *your* office and calling *you*. I don't think it was them. This crime has no note attached to it. This doesn't feel like a group making a statement but a single person acting out. I can investigate and see what's going on here."

Joe looked between Brady and me. "If whoever trashed Brady's hotel room is found and arrested, and I am assured that there are no other plans, then we could do the show without extra security. But what makes you think you can?"

"Don't you read Carson's holiday letters?" Brady asked Joe incredulously. I blushed a little. I love that my dad is proud of me, but it always makes me self-conscious that he includes updates on the cases I've solved in the letter he sends every year to our friends and family. "Nancy here is a detective," Brady continues. "She's solved loads of cases all around River Heights and even in other cities. Carson writes all about them."

"Oh . . . uh," Joe stammered.

"I've never solved a case in San Francisco, though," I said to Joe, who gave me a small embarrassed smile.

"I swear I read your father's letters. I just didn't put it together that you were the detective. I thought you were a lot older based on all your exploits." He looked at me for a second, thinking through his options. "You're sure you're up to the case?"

"I'm sure," I said. "Preventing sabotage is kind of my specialty."

"There is a lot of sabotage in River Heights," Ned said.

"All right, Nancy. You're on the case. Doors open for the show at seven p.m., so you need to have the culprit and I need to feel confident that you have discovered any other plans by six. Otherwise, I will call in the extra security."

Brady turned to me and looked me right in the eyes. "I'm counting on you, Nancy. The rest of my tour depends on you."

CHAPTER FOUR

Put a Button on It

"FOR THE RECORD, I'M NOT DOING THIS FOR your tour," I told Brady. "I do think you need to take some ownership of your actions. Even if you meant it as a joke, I don't think you should have called for violence against a heckler, and I think you should apologize. I'm taking this case because I don't want one of the first performances at the Arts Complex to be a disaster. It's too important to River Heights."

Brady looked like he wanted to argue, so I held up my hand to stop him. It was now almost one thirty, and Joe was giving me until six. We didn't have time to argue.

"First things first: we need to search this room," I said.

"What are we looking for?" Ned asked.

"Anything that looks out of place," I answered. "Whoever destroyed it must have exerted a lot of energy to do this level of damage. It's possible they dropped something or otherwise left something behind that will help us identify them."

"Okay. Where do we start?" asked Joe.

I surveyed the room. It was a good question. For a moment I felt overwhelmed by how much damage had been done. It could take a long time to go through everything, and I didn't have a lot of time before Joe would call in the extra security. It was also easy to imagine missing an important clue in the mess. But sometimes moving forward with one plan is better than waiting for the perfect plan.

I opened the door to the bathroom. It looked like that room had been left alone.

"Brady, is this how you left the bathroom?" I asked.

Brady peered in. "Yup, looks like they left that room alone."

"Okay, then we will too. Let's divide this room into quadrants," I said, "and each of us will be responsible for searching that quadrant. If there's anything that seems like it might be a clue, hold it up and Brady can tell us if it's his or not."

"You're lucky this is the first stop on my tour," Brady said.

"Why is that?"

"You won't be digging through my dirty laundry."

We all laughed.

"Okay," I said. "Brady, how about you take from the west wall through the left pillow, and then down the bottom of the bed. Joe, if you could take the east wall through the right pillow, Ned and I will split the space in front of the bed. Sound good?"

Everyone nodded and got to work.

I got down on my hands and knees and started in the upper left corner of my quadrant.

"Make sure you look under things. Even the smallest clue could help us find the person who did this," I reminded everyone as I focused my eyes intently down, looking for anything that seemed like it didn't belong to a middle-aged stand-up comic. I carefully shook out the pants that were strewn across my way. I was completely focused on the two square feet of carpet in front of me.

After a moment, Ned spoke up. "You know, these notebook pages aren't torn that small. I think we could put them back together."

"Don't tease me, Ned," Brady answered. "I can't take another disappointment right now."

"No, I'm serious," Ned said. "I'm pretty good at puzzles."

"He's being modest," I added. "He's *really* good at puzzles. It's a tradition in his family that they do a giant jigsaw puzzle every year over the holidays. And by 'giant' I mean like over five thousand pieces."

"Yeah, and we do the expert-level ones," Ned continued. "The ones that are approximately ninety percent sky or ocean, so each piece is blue with very little distinguishing it from the others."

I picked up a scrap of the notebook paper and examined it. It was about half an inch in size, but you could clearly make out the letters *st* on it. It wouldn't be easy to put it back together, but it was possible.

"I think he could do it," I said.

"Here," Ned said, taking the recording equipment out of its box. "Put all the notebook pieces you find in this box, and I will work on putting the pages back together after we finishing searching the room."

We got back to scouring our quadrants for clues, stopping only to put notebook scraps in the box. After a while my arms began to ache and my eyes started swimming from staying focused on a small spot for so long.

"There's nothing in my quadrant," Joe said, standing up and stretching his back.

"Mine either," said Brady.

"Sorry, Nancy," Ned chimed in. "I don't see anything either."

I hadn't had any luck either, and I was going to give up when suddenly my own words echoed in my head: *Look under things.*

"The bed," I said.

"Brady and Joe searched the bed," Ned said, confused.

"But they didn't search under it," I said. "Come on!" I lifted up the bed skirt, but it was too dark to see anything. I pulled out my phone, turned on its flashlight function, and shined it under the bed. I swept it from left to right, like I had seen the spotlights on police helicopters do on the news when they were searching for escaped suspects. The light caught something that flashed, but I couldn't make out what it was.

"There's something under there!" I exclaimed.

"What? What is it?" Brady asked, rushing to my side.

"I'm not sure," I said, stretching my arm underneath the bed. I reached as far as I could, but I still couldn't grasp it.

"Let me try," said Brady, shoving his arm under the bed. I watched him flail his arm, his face puckered in concentration, and I realized he was holding his breath.

"Got it!" he exclaimed, exhaling with a loud gasp.

He pulled his hand out, his fist clenched around the mystery object. Slowly he opened his fingers, revealing a large gold button about the size of a nickel with an anchor embossed on it, so it stood out from the button three-dimensionally.

"That looks like a button from a blazer," I said.

"Is it one of yours?" Ned asked Brady.

Brady laughed. "Did any of the clothes you saw strewn all over this room look like I would (a) wear a blazer or (b) wear anything that had an anchor on it?" He didn't wait for any of us to respond. "No, I am strictly a jeans and black T-shirt kind of guy. If it gets chilly, then perhaps I will don a black sweater."

"Then this is a clue!" Ned exclaimed. "Our culprit wore a blazer and lost a button!" I gave him a look, and Ned knew me well enough to know exactly what it meant.

"What?" Ned asked. "Why isn't this a clue?"

It was one of the things I liked best about my relationship with Ned—how well we could communicate without speaking.

"Well," I explained, "it's more that we don't know that it's a clue. This is a hotel room. For all we know, it belongs to a previous occupant."

"Then what was the point of spending half an hour crawling around on my hands and knees?" Joe asked huffily.

"It's still good," I said. "If we find someone in the course of our investigation who is missing an anchor button, we know that they're probably involved. We just can't rule anyone out because they don't have a blazer with a missing button."

Joe sighed. "I have to get back to my office. Brady, if you change your mind about the extra security, let me know. Nancy Drew, you have until six o'clock to convince me you have the suspect." He left the hotel room.

I felt bad that I hadn't convinced him that it wasn't a waste of time to search the room. Detective work isn't glamorous; there are a lot of dead ends and wrong theories before you solve the case, but each dead end is important, because it eliminates one possibility of what happened. It's just like taking a multiple-choice test: every answer that you know is wrong gets you closer to the right answer. I wish I had been able to explain better that just because we didn't know the button definitely *was* important, that didn't mean it definitely *wasn't*.

I turned to Ned. "I think it's time we go interview some of these members of RHVRA and see if they know anything."

Ned looked down at the box of notebook scraps we'd collected. "Do you mind seeing if George and Bess can go with you?" he asked. "It's just that I think putting this notebook back together could take a really long time, and I'd like to get started on it. Brady's going to help me."

"Sure," I replied. "That makes sense. But what about your interview for NED Talks?"

Ned glanced at Brady, who was on the other side of the room, gathering some of his belongings from the floor. "I think he might be open to answering some questions as we're working."

"Sure," I replied. "That makes sense."

"Thanks, Nancy," Ned said. "Let me know what you guys find."

"You got it. Good luck with your hardest puzzle yet," I told him before turning toward Brady. "Bye," I said. "I'll be in touch as soon as I have something to report."

"Thanks. Talk soon."

I stepped into the hall, pulled out my phone, and dialed George's number. She answered before the end of the first ring.

"Nancy!" she yelled so loudly that I had to pull the phone away from my ear. "I just finished my shift. How'd it go? Did my microphones work? Wait. Don't answer that. Bess is right here. I'm going to put you on speaker." After a moment, she said, "Okay, go ahead, you're on speaker."

"Well, the interview didn't happen yet, so I don't know how the mics worked."

"Oh no," Bess said. "Poor Ned. I know how much he was looking forward to this. Is he okay?" That was typical Bess. She is the kindest person I know and is always aware of other people's feelings and how events impact them.

"Yeah, he's okay, but we're on a case."

"What?!" Bess and George said in unison. Even though I wasn't with them, I knew they were both leaning into the phone excitedly. I may have the reputation for being a detective, but my friends have helped me on almost every case; they like solving mysteries about as much as I do.

"What do you need us to do?" George asked. A feeling of warmth spread through my body. It was such a relief to know that my friends always had my back. I knew that police officers and other detectives always worked with partners. I was lucky enough to have two partners. Three, if you counted Ned, but he was usually too busy with school stuff. I quickly explained what had happened and told them about the vandalized poster. I could hear George typing frantically in the background.

"I found the RHVRA website," George said. "It

says here they're holding a sit-in at Joe Archer's office at the Arts Complex."

"Yeah," I said. "That's where I'm headed."

"We'll meet you there," Bess said. "Don't go in without us." They hung up without saying goodbye, but I knew it was because they wanted to get there as fast as possible.

GEORGE AND BESS ARE IN, I texted to Ned as I walked back toward the elevators. Ned texted back a smiley face and wrote, WE GOT A PAGE PUT BACK TOGETHER IN THE NOTEBOOK.

As I rounded the corner, I spotted a housekeeper's cart outside a room. I took the button out of my pocket. I had an idea.

I approached the cart. I could hear the housekeeper working inside the room. I took a deep breath and knocked on the open door.

"Hello," I called out in a higher-pitched voice than I usually spoke in.

A gruff-looking middle-aged woman sporting a name tag that said PENELOPE came to the door, a cleaning rag in her hand. "I do the rooms in order," she said. "I'll get to your room when I get to it, so save your breath."

"Oh, no," I said cheerfully, "it's not about that. Well, it's kind of about that. My dad is staying in room 823, and he found this button on the floor." I held out my hand, showing her the button. "And it's such a nice button that we thought whoever the guest was who stayed in there before us might want it back. I was wondering if there was any way I could help get this button back to its owner?" I noticed that Penelope was staring at me with a suspicious look.

It felt a little ridiculous to make up an elaborate lie, but I wasn't ready to tell Penelope that the room had been destroyed. I wanted to preserve the crime scene as long as possible before involving the police. If she knew there'd been a break-in, she'd have to report it. I had hung the DO NOT DISTURB sign on the door handle for just that reason. At the same time, I did need to confirm whether this button was a real clue or a red herring.

"That room was perfectly clean. There was no button. What kind of scam is this?" she asked me harshly.

"I'm sorry?" I said. "I don't know what you mean." My mind raced. This was not the reaction I'd been expecting. My story had seemed pretty innocent to me and not something easy to refute. How did she know I was making this up?

"If you think you're going to get a free room by claiming the room wasn't cleaned properly, you have another think coming. Because I know that's a load of baloney."

"No, no. I really just want to return it to its owner, and I know that the people who clean the rooms know everything, so I thought I'd ask you. I can take it down to the front desk, of course."

"You will do no such thing," Penelope said. "I've read about people like you. You come into expensive hotels and find ways to get free rooms. I'm not falling for it."

I needed to change tactics. Penelope was wrong about the reason I was lying, but she definitely had cottoned to the fact that I wasn't telling the whole truth. I dropped my voice back down to its natural pitch. "I promise you I'm not trying to get a free room and I'm definitely not trying to get you in trouble, but I really did find this button in room 823. Why do you say that's impossible?"

"Because this floor was one of the last floors renovated. The guests staying in *these* rooms are the first guests to stay in them since the renovation. These rooms were spotless. Therefore you are lying, but I can take that button, if you want."

"No, that's okay. I think I'll hang on to it."

I thanked Penelope for her help and kept going toward the elevator. Bess and George would probably be at the Arts Complex by now. I needed to hurry to meet them. I could feel Penelope's eyes still on me as I made my way down the hall. Otherwise, I would have added a little skip to my step: the button could only have been left behind by the perpetrator. It was officially a clue!

CHAPTER FIVE

Sitting In

I HURRIED DOWN THE STREET TO THE ARTS Complex. Fortunately, it was only a few blocks from the hotel. As I got closer, I could see George and Bess standing outside. Waiting to cross the street, I took in the building itself. It had only been completed last month, but it was already one of my favorite buildings in River Heights. The city council had chosen an architect who specialized in modern and futuristic designs, and some people in River Heights had been skeptical. Everyone agreed that the final building was breathtaking, though. It was silver metal, seemingly composed of different-shaped buildings all stuck together. The largest piece jutted high into the sky. On a clear day, the sight of the silver against the bright blue sky was beautiful. The building did reflect the idea of the grandeur of the art.

"Nancy, come on," I heard George yell from across the street. I realized that I had gotten so lost in admiring the Arts Complex that I hadn't noticed the sign turn to WALK.

I crossed the street to join George and Bess.

"Sorry," I said. "I was just taking in the building."

"It really is great," George agreed.

"Yeah," Bess said. "I didn't think I would like it, but I really do." She's a traditionalist, and she had been dubious of the modern approach to the building.

"So, what's our mission, Nancy?" George asked.

I showed them the button. "We need to mingle among the protesters and see if one of them is missing a button that looks like this." I turned toward Bess. "I think George and I should be on distraction duty while you check out the clothes."

Bess nodded in agreement. Of the three of us, Bess knows the most about clothes. George is known for simplicity. Unless she's absolutely forced to dress up, she's never seen in anything other than jeans and a T-shirt. I have a slightly more varied wardrobe, and I don't hate clothes shopping the way George does, but fashion is not something I'm passionate about. Bess, on the other hand, loves clothes. She reads all the big style blogs and can tell you all about what was big at the fashion shows in Paris or New York. She always has the perfect outfit for any occasion.

Bess took the button from me and studied it scrupulously. "Anchors are a staple of preppy attire," she said. "We're probably going to be looking for someone who dresses in that style. Keep a particular eye out for people in boat shoes—those canvas loafers with leather laces—bright-colored pants, and collared shirts."

George and I nodded. "So what's our play going to be, Nancy?" George asked.

I grinned. "We're producers for NED Talks," I said.

Bess and George laughed. "If only Ned knew he

had three producers working on his podcast," George joked.

I opened the door to the complex and we stepped inside. It was just as beautiful as the outside. The walls were made of light-colored woods and a thin red carpet covered the floors. Wire sculptures of artists at work decorated the lobby: a ballet dancer in arabesque, a painter mid-brushstroke, a violinist strumming her instrument, an actor delivering a monologue. "Does anyone see a directory where we can find Joe Archer's office?" Bess asked.

"When I looked online, it said Joe's office was upstairs," George said, "but I don't see where the stairs are."

Two women holding signs that said VICTIMS' RIGHTS ARE NOT FUNNY passed us.

"I think we should follow them," I said.

"That's why you're the detective," George joked. We followed the women through the lobby to a door in the back right corner leading to a set of stairs. They turned as we went through the door behind them.

"Are you here for the sit-in?" one with curly hair and glasses asked.

"Yep," I said.

"That's great," her friend said. "Are you in one of Erica Vega's classes too?" she asked as we started up the stairs.

I looked between George and Bess. They looked as clueless as I did.

"Um, no," I said. "Who is Erica Vega?"

"Oh, she's amazing!" the curly-haired one enthused. "She's teaching this Politics of Art class here at the complex. It's incredible. She changed the whole way I think about art. She's the one who suggested we have this sit-in. I didn't know other people knew about it."

"Oh, I saw the group online," George jumped in. "I suggested that my friends come with me."

The women broke into excited grins. "That's great!" the one with curly hair said. "We didn't think anyone was paying attention. So far everyone who's shown up to sit in has been in Erica's class."

"Well, I was paying attention!" George said.

"Cool, I'm glad our cause is spreading," the woman said. We had reached the top of the stairs, and they led us through another door, which deposited us in a typical office-building hallway. It was much different from the downstairs area. The only thing that distinguished it from being a building that housed accountants or lawyers was that the hallways were adorned with stenciled paintings of musical notes, ballet shoes, the tragedy and comedy masks, and paintbrushes.

We were standing directly in front of an office door with a nameplate that said JOE ARCHER in big letters. We could hear the murmur of a group of people inside but couldn't make out any of the words.

We followed the women into the waiting area of Joe's office. The small space was packed with at least fifty people. Almost all of them were women. Many of them were holding signs. The door shut behind us, and we were squeezed up against the wall with barely any room to maneuver. Sweat had already started beading on my forehead from all the body heat in the room. At a desk in the corner, a woman who I assumed was Joe's assistant tried to work in the chaos. Behind her was the door to Joe's office. Through the din, I could hear a rhythmic clacking sound coming from inside.

"What is that noise?" I asked.

"I think it's a typewriter! I read an interview with him, and he mentioned that he can't get used to a computer keyboard," Bess exclaimed after a moment.

"That's crazy!" George exclaimed. "I thought nobody had used a typewriter in decades."

I laughed. "Well, I guess one person still does. But back to the case. Bess, do you see anything?"

Bess looked at a loss. With the room so full, it was impossible for her to get a good look at anyone's clothes. It was time for me to do my thing.

"Excuse me," I said. One woman standing a few feet from me turned her head in my direction, but the rest of the women ignored me. I tried again, louder. "Excuse me!" A few more heads turned my way. I tried again, really yelling this time. "EXCUSE ME!" The room went suddenly quiet, and now everyone was looking at me.

I cleared my throat. "Hi," I said. "I'm a producer with NED Talks, which is an up-and-coming podcast. Our host, Ned Nickerson, is interviewing Brady Owens." Immediately, everyone started booing. "And we want to hear your side!" I said before the boos got too loud and I lost them. They simmered down. "Ned wants to make sure both perspectives are represented. My coproducer and I," I said, indicating George, "will be conducting pre-interviews for potential guests on the show." I paused dramatically. "Who would like to be considered as a guest?" Everyone in the room shot up their hands.

"Is Ned really going to interview one of them?" George whispered in my ear.

"Of course. He's a responsible journalist. He'll want to get both sides of this story," I whispered back.

"Great," I said to the whole group. "George and I will begin circulating and asking questions about your viewpoint."

I approached the woman in front of me, and the others lined up behind her, creating more space in the room. Bess nodded and started floating toward the back.

"What's your name?" I asked.

"I'm Jennifer," she answered. I pulled out a small reporter's notebook that I always carry with me in case a situation like this pops up and I need to write down clues. It's long and skinny, so I can easily hold it in one hand to take notes. It's old-fashioned and George makes fun of me for not just using my phone, but I find it much easier and faster.

"So, why are you here? Why do you think a meeting with Joe Archer is important?"

"We feel strongly that he should cancel Brady Owens's performance. Brady crossed the line when he advocated violence, and the River Heights Arts Complex should not condone that kind of behavior."

"But what about free speech?" George asked. "Doesn't the First Amendment say that Brady has the right to say whatever he wants?"

Another woman jumped out of line and stood next to Jennifer. "Of course. Brady has that right," she argued. "The First Amendment just says the government can't tell Brady what he can and cannot say. The Arts Complex is a private business. It can decide who it does and doesn't want to support." She looked at me. "My name is Corinne, by the way, if you want to write that down."

"And," Jennifer continued, "we have the right to say that we don't agree. We just wish Joe Archer would actually listen us. He pushes past us without listening every time he goes to his office. Like just now. The River Heights Arts Complex is really important to all of us and he should hear what we have to say."

I nodded and jotted down what she'd just said. I stole a glance at Bess, who was circulating among the group, appraising their outfits and snapping photos on her phone.

"Exactly," Corinne added. "Brady can say whatever he wants, but that doesn't mean there aren't consequences. And in my book, the penalty for suggesting that an audience of over two hundred people mug a single woman in a dark parking lot is that you don't get to be paid to tell jokes anymore." She paused, and I saw her discreetly wipe a tear away.

"Are you all right?" I asked.

"Sorry," she said. "I was mugged a few months ago as I was walking home from school. One man grabbed me from behind while another one snatched my purse. It was the scariest moment of my life. I had bruises on my arms for weeks from where he grabbed me, and I'm lucky I wasn't more seriously hurt. So the idea that this comedian thinks he can make a joke about that and urge people to commit that crime . . . it makes me really angry."

I nodded and thanked her for telling me her story. It may have only been a ruse when I had said we were pre-interviewing people for Ned's show, but now I knew how important it was to have a few of these protesters on the podcast. It was an important issue, and they had important things to say.

In the meantime, though, I still had a job to do.

"How long have you been conducting this sit-in?" I asked.

"We've had people here for more than a week," Jennifer said.

"Yeah, and Joe Archer hasn't even deigned to meet with us," Corinne said loudly, throwing her voice in the direction of Joe's assistant. The assistant looked up at Corinne and then pointedly lowered her eyes again, ignoring her.

"Brady goes on at seven o'clock tonight. At this point, it seems like Joe Archer is not going to give in to your request to cancel the show. Do you have a plan B?"

Jennifer and Corinne exchanged looks, and I caught Jennifer ever so slightly shaking her head no at Corinne.

"Nope. This is it. There's no plan B."

I was pretty sure they were lying, but before I could press them any further, the door to the hallway swung open, and a tall woman with dark hair and bright blue eyes stood in the doorway. She was wearing creased gray slacks and a white shirt with an argyle V-neck sweater vest over it. Her face glistened with sweat, her hair was disheveled, and her shirt was wrinkled. Still, she was a commanding presence, and immediately everyone's attention shot to her.

"Tami! You're back!" Jennifer cried next to me.

There was a pregnant pause as everyone waited for Tami to respond.

"The eagle has landed! The petitions have been delivered!" Tami yelled, and broke out into a wide smile. Everyone in the room flocked around her, effectively boxing me, George, and Bess out of the group to the outskirts.

Bess came up next to me. I turned toward her. "I know I'm not a fashion expert, but her clothes meet the definition of preppy, right?"

Bess nodded. "Definitely. And those pants could be the bottom half of a pantsuit, the top half of which would be a blazer."

I looked back at Tami. I could barely make her out among all the other activists encircling her.

I shoved myself past Jennifer and Corinne to the center of the circle, so I was right next to Tami.

"Hi. Tami, right?"

"Yeah. Who are you?"

"I'm Nancy. I'm a producer for the NED Talks podcast, and I just wanted to say that I love your outfit."

"Okay. Thanks?" she said, clearly confused as to why I was bringing this up. I had to admit, it wasn't the smoothest line of questioning I had ever done in my days of being a detective, but sometimes you just had to go for it.

"Anyway, I'm in the market for a new blazer, and I'd really love one with gold buttons. Oh, and I'm a big fan of anchors. Do you know where I could get something like that?"

Tami looked at me like I was crazy. "Um, I am in the middle of something much more important than giving out fashion advice." She turned toward the group. "Listen up, ladies. We are stopping this performance by any means necessary!"

CHAPTER SIX

An Unsettling Discovery

EVERYONE IN THE ROOM CHEERED.

"How are you going to do that?" I asked, but no one responded. In fact, I got the impression that I was being deliberately ignored. "We'd love to have one of you on our podcast discussing your plans," I tried.

The circle around Tami was tight, and there were frantic whispers going back and forth, but aside from the odd word, like "boycott" and "protest," I couldn't make anything out.

I turned back to George and Bess and pointed toward the door. "Let's go," I said.

The hallway felt like a cool relief when we stepped out of the overly crowded office.

"Oh, thank goodness! I can breathe again!" George crowed dramatically. "I thought I was going to suffocate in there."

"It wasn't that bad," Bess said, wiping sweat from her forehead with a handkerchief. "Okay, maybe it was," she corrected herself, seeing how wet her hankie was.

"All right, Nancy," George said. "What's next?"

"Well, Tami's definitely on the suspect list. She wore the right type of clothes and she looked like she had physically exerted herself, but we need more proof before we move forward with any accusations. I think we should go and check out that teacher, Erica Vega," I said.

"Makes sense to me," said Bess. "It seems like she's the one really inspiring these people to protest." She paused, then added, "You know, I feel like I've heard the name Erica Vega before, but I can't remember from where."

"Well, according to this schedule online, she's teaching a class right now!" George said, looking at her phone. "It looks like the classroom is just down this hall, too."

We started walking down the hallway. As we were heading that way, we passed a sign pointing to the museum.

"Oh, Bess, I forgot to tell you," I said. "They're having a Dutch masters exhibit here. It opens this weekend. Here, I took a photo of the poster for you."

I handed her my phone with the photo on it.

"Oh, wow!" Bess said. "This is amazing. It says they're going to be showing *The Zebra Finch*, which is incredible."

"Why?" George asked.

"Well, it's supposed to be beautiful, and the detail of the light on the bird's feathers is really intricate, but the big thing about it is that it's part of a private collection and the owner almost never lets it be shown. I think it's only been exhibited two or three times in the thirty years that she's owned it. I didn't think I'd ever get to see it, and it's coming right to River Heights!"

"Well, we'll definitely have to go," I said.

We kept walking.

"It really is neat how the classrooms and performance spaces are all in this one building," George said.

I agreed. "Which is why we need it to be successful and not have Brady's performance sabotaged."

"Classroom 17. This is it," George said, pointing to the door.

I put my ear up against the door. I could hear a woman lecturing. "Let's go for it," I said.

I creaked open the door. The classroom was a lecture hall with stadium-style seating. At the front was a woman with short blond hair holding court.

"Freedom of expression comes with responsibilities," Erica said.

I pushed the door open farther, and Erica stopped talking to look up at us.

"Sorry," I said. "I was hoping we could sit in."

"Yeah, yeah. Come in. Come in. Quickly."

Bess, George, and I found seats in the back and slid in as quietly as we could.

"Artists and performers they think that they are a protected class. They think they can say whatever they want and they are covered by the fact that they make 'art.' But that is not the case. Artists don't get a blank check where they can offend anyone they want and not get called out for it."

Erica was speaking more and more loudly. As I looked around the room, I observed that the attendees were rapt at what she was saying. I saw several people nodding their heads along with her.

"Artists need to be held accountable. And who do you think needs to hold them accountable?"

Several hands shot up in the air.

"Kristen," Erica said, pointing to a young woman in the front.

"The people!" Kristen said enthusiastically.

"That's right!" Erica said. "The people! When an artist crosses the line, the people have to tell him or her. And how do they do that? Don't bother raising your hands. Just shout it out."

"Boycotting!" someone yelled.

"Organizing on social media!" someone else shouted.

"Protesting!"

"Showing them what it feels like!"

"Yes! Yes! Yes!" Erica said. "You do what you have to do to get your point heard." She checked her watch. "All right. That's all we have time for this week. Good luck tonight. Go out there and fight the good fight."

"Will we see you tonight protesting the show?" a student asked.

"Unfortunately, I have somewhere else I need to be tonight," Erica said, "but I will be there with you in spirit."

The students filed out and Bess, George, and I pushed to the front of the room to talk to Erica.

"Hey, Nancy," Bess whispered. "Do you mind if I take the lead on talking to her?" I looked at Bess in surprise. She is always a great help in my investigations, but she rarely asks to take the lead. She nodded at me, looking more determined than I'd ever seen her.

"Okay," I agreed.

"Ms. Vega," Bess said. "I'm Bess Marvin, and I just wanted to say I'm a big fan."

Erica Vega raised her eyebrows and waited for Bess to go on. George and I looked at Bess, wondering what she was up to.

"I really loved the blog entry you wrote about *The Zebra Finch*," Bess continued. "I thought your analysis of the brushstrokes was genius."

"Thanks," Erica said, sounding genuinely impressed. "I haven't met many people who have read that article."

"It's one of my favorite paintings of all time. I read everything I can about it. I can't believe I'm finally going to get to see it in person in River Heights!"

"It's an amazing thing to see in real life," she said. "If you'll forgive me, I need to run."

I looked down and noticed she was pulling a rolling suitcase.

"Oh, are you headed to the airport?" I asked.

"No, I have a meeting," she said.

I pushed forward. "I don't want to hold you up, but we're producers for a podcast and we're looking for protesters to interview. Could you recommend any of your students?" I asked. "Who's leading the charge here?"

"Oh, that's easy," Erica said. "Tami Wright. She's my star student, and she would be very articulate about her views. All the students look up to her. Now, I'm sorry, but I really need to run."

She headed out, leaving me and my friends alone in the lecture hall.

"Wow. She is intense," George said. "But, Bess, you were genius!"

"Thanks," said Bess. "It kept bugging me why I thought I knew her name, and then it hit me."

"You were great," I agreed. "Tami is definitely our prime suspect."

My phone buzzed in my pocket. I pulled it out to see a text from Ned: TAKING A BREAK FROM WORKING WITH BRADY. WANT TO MEET UP?

I checked with Bess and George and then texted him back. SURE. SEE YOU OUTSIDE ARTS COMPLEX IN 5 MINUTES?

Ned agreed, and Bess, George, and I slipped out of the lecture hall and made our way back out to the street, where I saw Ned rounding the corner.

"Hey, how'd it go with Brady?" I asked him.

"We made some progress. We got two pages of the notebook put back together. I don't know if he'll ever get it all back, but at least he'll have some. The good news is he let me do the interview with him as a distraction while we were working on it."

"That's great!" I said. "How was it?"

"I think it went really well. Because he was working on this other task, I think he was more open with me in his answers than he would have been otherwise." That made sense to me. I always liked when someone I was interviewing for a case was doing something else while we were chatting. They tended to be less guarded and more careless with their words.

"In fact, would you guys mind if we went somewhere so I could back up the interview? It's too good. I don't want to risk only having it on my computer," Ned said.

"Can we do that somewhere there is food?" George asked. "I didn't eat lunch and I'm starving."

I checked my watch. We'd already investigated for an hour and we'd made some progress, but I didn't feel close to solving the case. I was going to argue that we push on, but the look on George's and Ned's faces told me that I needed to take this break if I wanted them working at their peaks. George was no good to me if she fainted from hunger, and Ned wouldn't be able to focus if he was worried about losing his interview. "My house is closest," I said. "I'm sure Hannah can make us something." Hannah Gruen is our housekeeper. She's been taking care of my dad and me since my mom passed away when I was little. She is, among other things, the best cook in River Heights, so my friends agreed readily.

I called ahead to let Hannah know we were coming, and fifteen minutes later, we walked in the door to find four turkey sandwiches sitting on the kitchen table. Not only that, but they were each made exactly how we liked them. Mine had no lettuce. The crusts were cut off George's. Ned's had extra mustard. And Bess's had cheddar instead of swiss.

I gave Hannah a hug and thanked her. Ned set up his interview to download off the recorder and joined us at the table.

Just as we started eating, my dad walked into the kitchen. I was surprised to see him home on a weekday. His eyes were glassy and his nose was red.

"Hi, Dad. Your allergies acting up?" I asked.

"Yeah. Kerri told me my sneezes were distracting the entire office and ordered me home." Kerri was my dad's assistant, and like Hannah, she didn't let the fact that she worked for my dad stop her from bossing him around.

"How'd the interview go, Ned?" my dad asked, sniffling loudly.

"Well . . . it was a little more dramatic than I had expected," Ned answered. We quickly filled him in on everything that had gone on.

"Wow. Brady just can't stay out of trouble. Typical Brady, though, to stick his foot in his mouth by calling out that heckler the way he did."

"But don't you think his job as a stand-up comedian is to push boundaries?" Ned asked.

"Well, tell me, what boundary was Brady pushing?" my dad asked Ned.

Ned opened his mouth to answer but quickly shut it, as he tried to think of what to say. I contemplated too. I believed that art should make people uncomfortable, but I also couldn't answer my dad's question.

"He wasn't pushing any boundary," Bess said. "He was just being a bully."

"Exactly," my dad said. "When you tell a joke that hits at someone, you want to punch up. You want the punch line to land against someone more powerful than you. If you call out or make fun of someone with less power than you, you're just being mean. You're not making a point." We were all quiet for a moment before my dad continued. "I don't think Brady is a bad person. I think he's sensitive and he got upset at the heckler and he lashed out. Then it all spiraled out of control."

"Okay, even if he did make a mistake, that doesn't

mean people should destroy his room or call for violence against him on Twitter," George argued.

"No, of course not," my dad said. "People have
every right to protest his show and tell him why they're
upset, but they definitely crossed a line."

"Plus, it's just not productive," I said. "Brady is so
upset about what's happening to him, he's not listening
to hear that they might have a point."

"I wish people could just talk calmly to each other,"
Bess said. "So many misunderstandings could be
avoided."

"But then there would be way fewer mysteries to
solve!" I joked. I've had a lot of cases where the motive
came down to wanting revenge for a perceived slight.

"Hey, was Joe cackling with glee at Brady's misfortune?" my dad asked.

"No. Why would he? I thought they were friends,"
I answered.

My dad started laughing, and pretty soon he was
laughing so hard he was coughing. Hannah came over
with a glass of water for him.

"You need to take care of yourself," she reprimanded him.

"I'm not sick," my dad protested. "It's just allergies."

Hannah shook her head.

"No, they are not friends at all," my dad said, getting back to his story. "They've been feuding since our days in the fraternity. I was shocked when I saw that Brady was going to perform at the Arts Complex."

My dad turned to Ned. "Didn't I tell you all this when I connected you to Brady?"

Ned blushed. "You were in the middle of the McKnight trial. You kind of just grunted and handed me a slip of paper with Brady's e-mail on it. I didn't want to bother you by asking any questions."

"Huh," my dad said. "That was a beast of a trial."

"So, what happened between them?" I asked.

"Every year our fraternity hosted an open mic, and we'd invite all the alumni. It was one of our biggest events of the year. We all took it really seriously. I did my Elvis impression, of course."

I couldn't help but roll my eyes. My dad was very

proud of his impression of Elvis Presley. He went all in, too. He lowered his voice, shook his hips, and lifted just one side of his lip. It was very goofy. I just hoped he wouldn't do it now. It was one thing for my dad to put on that performance in front of Hannah and me. It was a whole other thing for him to do it for my friends, not to mention my boyfriend.

My dad liked to embarrass me, but he also knew I was on a case and that we didn't have time to waste.

"Both Brady and Joe did stand-up comedy sets their junior year, but about seventy-five percent of their jokes were the same. They were roommates, and Joe accused Brady of stealing his jokes. Brady went before Joe, so Joe's set completely bombed, since the jokes were similar. If I recall correctly, he even got booed. He was furious. Brady claimed it was coincidental."

Hannah put a plate of chocolate chip cookies on the kitchen table, and Ned lit up. Hannah's cookies were his favorite—a fact he never told his grandmother.

"I have an extra bag for you to take back with you to the dorms," Hannah told him. Ned got up and engulfed her in a hug. It was comical how much taller he was than her.

"You're the best," he told Hannah.

"Who did you believe?" I asked as Ned sat back down. I was anxious to get back to the story.

"I was never sure. It was possible that it was a coincidence. Most of the jokes were about life in the fraternity and on campus, which were experiences they both had. At the same time, they were very similar, and we all knew Brady was extremely competitive and would do anything to win. Before the open mic incident, he almost got kicked out of our fraternity when he cheated during a track-and-field competition we had among all the frats on campus. His event was the half mile, and he got caught taking a shortcut."

"What happened after the open mic?" Ned asked.

"Well, it turned out that Jack Murray, who was an alumnus and a big talent agent, was in the audience that night. He thought that Brady had big potential and signed him to his agency, so Brady's career basically started that night. Joe was furious. He believed that Jack might have signed him if he'd performed before Brady."

My dad paused to take a bite of a cookie.

"I wasn't so sure," he continued. "Even though the jokes were similar, Brady's delivery was indisputably better than Joe's. His timing was impeccable. He knew exactly when to pause, what word to emphasize to get the biggest laugh. He was just a natural in a way I don't think Joe was. When Joe was up there, you could see the gears turning in his head as he thought about how to make the joke as funny as possible. Joe's a very smart guy, but he was awkward onstage. Joe was so mad, he moved out of their room and slept on the couch in the living room. Brady ended up dropping out a few weeks later to pursue being a comic full-time." He stopped and looked each one of us in the eyes. "Something none of you kids will ever, ever do. When you get to college, you will stay there and you will graduate."

We all nodded and promised that we would stay in school. Of course, none of us were considering dropping out of school, but if it made my dad happier to hear us say it out loud, then we would.

"I didn't think Joe and Brady had spoken to each other since Brady left college, which was close to twenty years ago now. I stayed in touch with both of them. Since I didn't know what happened, I didn't want to take sides, and they're both nice guys in their own ways." He took another bite of his cookie and shrugged. "But, you know, Joe's done very well in his career, and it was a better fit for him anyway."

I turned and exchanged a look with my friends. Maybe Joe was a suspect.

My dad put his glass of water down with a *thunk*. "Nancy, no," he said, immediately knowing what I was thinking. "This was a long time ago, when we were practically kids. When I asked if Joe was happy to see Brady's misfortune, I didn't mean to imply that he was involved personally. Just that he might think karma had a long memory."

"Okay, Dad. I get it," I said.

My dad nodded and checked his watch. "Oh, good

grief," he said. "I've got to get back to work. I have a brief due to a judge in three hours." He got up and kissed me on top of my head. "Good luck with the case." He waved to my friends before taking another cookie and heading down the hall to his home office. "Good to see you all. I'll see you at the show tonight."

He turned to me one last time. "I'm serious. Joe's not a suspect."

I watched him walk down the hall and then turned back to my friends.

"Obviously he *is* a suspect," I said.

CHAPTER SEVEN

Insecure Security

"I MEAN, RIPPING UP HIS NOTEBOOK WITH all his jokes would definitely be good revenge for Brady stealing his jokes," Ned said.

"Yeah, and if you think about it, Joe is the one who determines whether I solve the case to his satisfaction," I said. "I could bring him a suspect and he could say I don't have enough evidence, so he would still add security or even cancel the show if he thought it was too big a risk."

"It's a really long time to wait to get that revenge," Bess pointed out. "Do you think he still cares?"

"That's true," I agreed. "It does seem a little odd for someone Joe's age to care this much about a college fight."

"We don't know how much Joe really wanted to be a stand-up comedian," George said. "Maybe, even though he's been successful, he's felt like a failure because he didn't accomplish his real dream."

"Yeah, but Nancy, we saw Joe eating with Brady in the hotel restaurant," Ned said. "How could he have trashed Brady's room?"

I felt like my head was swimming. I sighed and checked my watch. I had been investigating the case for two hours and had only two and a half hours left before the cutoff Joe had given me. I didn't know the best way forward. Tami and Erica seemed like viable suspects, but so did Joe.

"We need more information," I announced. "We rushed into thinking that this was about Brady's mugging jokes. We didn't think about the possibility that there was another motive. We need to take a step back and assess what we know about Brady." I turned to

Ned. "And we need to get a full timeline from Brady. We have no idea when he left his room or when it was trashed. We've just been assuming that it was while he and Joe were having lunch, but we don't know."

I sighed again. I had launched so directly into this case that I hadn't stopped to consider all the angles. I had been working off assumptions rather than facts. These were rookie mistakes, and I should know better.

As if reading my mind, Ned put his hand on my shoulder. "I know you're beating yourself up, Nancy, but you shouldn't. You pursued the most logical lead first."

"Yeah," George agreed. "And Tami could still be the culprit. We haven't ruled her out."

"I know," I said. "This case is just so important. The town has put so much money into this Arts Complex, and so many businesses are counting on it being a success," I said. "I just want to make sure I get it right."

"You'll solve it," said Bess, giving me her most supportive smile. "You have three solid leads and more than two hours."

"Yeah," George said. "That's plenty of time."

I took a deep breath and set my jaw. My friends were right. I was going to solve this case, but I wasn't going to do it by sitting around feeling sorry for myself.

I stood up quickly, pushing my chair out so forcefully I almost knocked it over, much to Hannah's disapproval. "We need to talk to Brady and get the whole story," I said.

We thanked Hannah for lunch and headed back out.

Fifteen minutes later Bess, George, Ned, and I strode through the lobby of the Towering Heights Resort, heading straight to Brady's room. I caught our reflections in the elevator; we looked like a team of undercover superheroes off to save the day. Without a word, we rode the elevator and marched down the hall to Brady's room, where I knocked authoritatively on the door.

"It's not locked," Brady said meekly from inside.

I opened the door to find Brady curled up in a ball on his bed. He looked terrible. He was ashen, and I was pretty sure he had been crying. He looked like a pale imitation of the high-energy, fast-talking man we had met earlier in the day.

Ned rushed to his side. "Brady? Are you okay? Nancy needs to ask you some questions."

"What's the point?" Brady asked, not even bothering to lift his head from the pillow. "It's going to be a disaster. This whole tour is going to be a disaster."

"That's not true," Ned said. "Nancy's on the case. We're going to solve this."

"All the work I've done for the past year is destroyed and my career is in the hands of a teenage detective. That's how far I've fallen!" He pulled the pillow over his head.

Bess stepped forward and yanked the pillow off Brady's head.

"Mr. Owens, we haven't met, but my name is Bess Marvin. I am helping Nancy with your case, but she can't solve it without your help. We have a little over two hours to figure out who targeted you. We're not giving up and neither should you, as you have a lot more to lose than we do. So sit up, clean yourself up, and answer Nancy's questions."

Brady opened one eye and saw Bess glowering down at him sternly. When Bess means business, you don't want to mess with her. Brady obviously agreed, because after a moment he grudgingly sat up.

"Give me a minute," he grumbled as he trudged to the bathroom. We heard water running.

"Thank you," I said quietly to Bess.

She shrugged. "Sometimes people just need a little tough love."

"And you always know when!" I said.

Brady emerged from the bathroom, his face freshly scrubbed and his hair combed back. He looked calmer and more clear-eyed.

"Okay, Nancy, go ahead and shoot," he said, sitting down in a chair across from me. I propped myself on the edge of the bed.

"Okay, first for the easy part. Can you walk us through your timeline of the day? When did you leave your room?"

"I left my room around eleven a.m. and went for a walk into town. I was feeling a little jet-lagged and wanted to get some fresh air before lunch."

"And what time did you meet Joe?"

"I met Joe a little past noon."

"Did you go back to your room in between?"

Brady shook his head. "I had planned to, but Joe was waiting for me in the lobby when I got back, so I didn't have time."

I nodded. "We got to the room . . ."

"Exactly at one o'clock," Ned finished.

"So, that's a two-hour window for our culprit to have entered the room." I looked over at George, who was dutifully typing notes into her phone.

I turned back to Brady and cleared my throat, shifting uncomfortably on the bed. There was no easy way to bring up what I was going to ask next.

"We heard that you and Joe got into a fight in college . . . ," I started.

"Oh, for goodness' sake!" Brady shouted before catching himself and taking a deep breath. "That was a misunderstanding. I did not steal his jokes. Besides," he continued, "we mended those fences a long time ago."

"Really?" I asked. "That's not what I heard."

"It's not like we sent out an announcement saying we were talking again, but a few years ago, I had a show in San Francisco and Joe came. We caught up and we put it all behind us."

I nodded. "Is there anyone else who has accused you of stealing jokes?" I asked.

"No! I don't steal jokes!" Brady bellowed. "If I stole jokes, why would I be so upset that my notebook was destroyed? I would just go out and steal some more! And if this is the path you're going down in this 'investigation,'" he sneered, "then I might as well call Joe up and cancel my show right now, because you ain't never going to solve this thing."

"As a detective, I have to follow all leads," I said coolly. It wasn't the first time I had been yelled at by a client. Sometimes the digging around you did in a person's life led you to discover some things they would rather you didn't, but as a detective my focus was on the truth, no matter how uncomfortable. Besides, even if it wasn't pleasant to have Brady shout at me, I was happy that he was getting back to his old self. It had been disconcerting to see him so down and broken.

"Well, I'm telling you this is the wrong lead," Brady insisted. "Stick to that two-hour window."

I turned toward George. "I need to see the hotel's security footage of the lobby." She nodded.

My friends immediately jumped into action.

"Are you thinking a distract and delay?" Ned asked me.

I nodded.

"We know what to do," Bess said.

"I don't know what to do," Brady protested. "What are we doing?"

"We'll fill you in," said Ned. "You can go, Nancy. We got this."

George and I headed back down to the lobby.

I spotted a door marked STAFF ONLY in the back right corner. I pointed it out to George. "They'll probably come out through there."

George nodded. She grabbed a cup of water from the cooler in the center of the room and sauntered over to the staff-only door. She leaned up against the wall, looking nonchalant as she sipped water and scrolled on her phone.

She met my eyes, indicating that she was set.

I stepped outside the lobby and pulled out my phone and dialed the number of the hotel.

"Towering Heights Resort. This is Pete speaking. How may I direct your call?"

"Pete, it's Nancy Drew."

"Hey, Nancy. Did you find Brady Owens?" he asked.

"I did. Remember how you said you owed me a favor because I got Jake back for you?"

"Sure," Pete answered.

"I need to cash that in. First, how many security guards are on duty right now?"

"Well, actually," Pete said, "they're still in the processing of hiring people post-renovation and are a little short-staffed. There are only two on during the day."

"Great. Also, can you patch my call through to security and tell them I'm a guest in room 823?"

"What's going on, Nancy?"

"The less you know, the better," I said. "Can you please just do this for me?"

There was a long pause, and I was suddenly worried that Pete would say no. I hadn't considered that Pete wouldn't help. I had been sure I could count on him.

Suddenly the phone was ringing.

"Hotel security," a gruff voice answered. Pete had come through after all!

"Security! Come quick. I just got back to my room and saw two men go running out and when I stepped inside, the room had been completely destroyed and my grandmother's diamond engagement ring is missing."

"We'll send someone right away," the voice said, bored. "You're in room 823?"

"Yes, but some*one*?!" I shrieked, really emphasizing the "one" to make my point. "Did you not hear what I just said?! There are two men on the run in your hotel, one of whom has my grandmother's diamond engagement ring. You need to send two officers. At least."

"All right, ma'am, we're on our way." I heard rustling sounds, as if he was standing up, right before the phone hung up.

I dashed back into the hotel, making a beeline for the staff-only door. George was gone.

I knocked softly on the door and heard it unlatch. With a quick glance over my shoulder, I slipped in.

George was waiting for me on the other side.

"How many officers did you see leave?" I asked her.

"Two," she answered.

"Phew. I can't believe that worked. Sometimes you really do get lucky. Hopefully Ned, Bess, and Brady can keep them occupied for a bit."

"The security office is down this way," George said.

"Head up, shoulders back," I told George.

"I know, I know," she answered impatiently, as we proceeded confidently down the hall. Long ago I had learned that if you looked like you belonged somewhere, people rarely questioned you. George's tone suggested I had imparted this lesson to my friends once or twice.

We got to the office marked SECURITY. I peered in.

"It's all clear," I told George.

We slipped inside and George went straight to the computer. Within a few minutes she had the security camera footage up on the monitor.

"I don't understand how you always know just what to do," I said, marveling.

"The machines . . . they talk to me," George joked. "Hang on. I've almost got it set back to eleven o'clock." She entered a few more strokes. "Okay, here's Brady leaving the building. Let's start watching from here."

On the monitor were six smaller squares, each with a different angle on the lobby.

"You take the top row, I'll take the bottom?" I asked.

"Sure," replied George. "I'm going to set it to eight times speed so we can get through as much of it as possible before the security guys come back. So, um, don't blink."

George hit play, and the footage started moving

absurdly fast. Between the speed and the fact that it was in black and white, I felt like I was watching an old silent film. I kept my eyes regularly scanning between my three assigned cameras. At this speed, it was more about looking for anything that jumped out than really following what was going on. For the most part it was just footage of people walking to or from the reception desk or the elevators.

"There's Joe!" I said, pointing at the upper right corner. "Slow it down."

George reduced the speed to its normal rate, which now felt like we were watching the footage in extreme slow motion.

"He's heading toward the elevators," George said.

"That's weird. Brady said he met Joe in the lobby." On the screen, Joe stepped into the elevator. "Can you zoom in, so we can see what floor it goes up to?"

George clicked on the screen and it zoomed into the top of the elevator where it displayed what floor the elevator was on. We watched it go up the floors: two, three, four, five, six, seven, eight.

"That's pretty damning evidence," George said.

"Let's see how long he stays up there. It took time to destroy that room. If he comes down in a minute or two, we can rule him out."

George nodded and sped up the footage again. I kept my eyes on the elevator.

"Wait, there's Tami!" George yelped.

I looked down at her row, and sure enough there was Tami.

"So she definitely came to the hotel," I said.

"Yeah," George said. "And she's heading toward the elevators too!"

"Who's that?" I asked George, pointing to a man who had entered behind Tami. He was wearing a suit with a plain black baseball cap, and I thought I could make out the edge of sunglasses underneath the bill. I couldn't put my finger on it, but there was something about his body language that made me feel like something was off about him. If I had more time, I could figure it out, but we only had two hours left.

"I don't know," George said. "I can't see his face."

"Yeah," I said, as I scanned all six of the cameras, but his face was obscured on all the cameras. "That's weird."

"I'm sure it's just a coincidence," George said. "Look, there's Joe getting out of the elevator."

I checked the time stamp on the footage. "He was up there for twenty minutes. That's definitely enough time to have trashed the room," I said.

"And Tami's still up there," George added.

My eye drifted back to the man in the baseball cap, but before I could watch him any further, my phone buzzed. It was a text from Bess.

"Security is on their way back down." Suddenly I noticed the time she had sent it. "Oh, no. She sent this six minutes ago. I only have one bar down here. It must not have gone through right away. They'll be here any second."

All of a sudden there was a rattle at the door.

"Who locked this door?" the same gruff voice I had spoken to on the phone grumbled.

CHAPTER EIGHT

Tweet Storm

THE DOOR HANDLE RATTLED AGAIN.

"James, do you have your keys?" the gruff voice asked.

"Yeah, hang on one second."

"What do we do?" George asked frantically.

I cast my eyes around the room feverishly, looking for a solution. The room was sterile and white. There were no closets or piles of boxes we could hide behind, and even if there were, who knows how long we would be stuck there?

My eyes landed on the window. It was half-open,

and I was confident we could both slip out of it. It was a good eight feet above the floor, but if we pushed the chair over, we could reach it.

I could hear footsteps coming down the hallway, and keys jingling.

"Nancy!" George hissed.

I pointed at the window. She nodded. As quickly and as quietly as we could, we slid the chair over to the wall.

"You go first," I whispered to George.

George climbed on the chair and hoisted herself into the frame. She looked back at me momentarily and then jumped out. I heard her hit the ground with a *thud*. My turn.

I stood on top of the chair and reached up to the sill. I heard the keys enter the lock. In another few seconds, they would be inside the room. I lightly jumped off the chair and pulled myself up onto the sill. I had jumped too hard and propelled myself half out the window.

We were higher off the ground than I'd realized. I

saw George standing on the open ground below, beckoning me. I started to feel a little dizzy. This was a much farther fall than I had expected.

Behind me, the lock turned. There was no time to think. I pushed myself forward. My stomach dropped as I hurtled through the air. As soon as I hit the ground, I tucked into a ball and rolled, just as I had been taught to do in PE class. When I stopped moving, I felt dizzy and the wind had been knocked out of me, making it hard to breathe.

"Hey someone's been in here!" one of the security officers bellowed from inside the office. Above me, the window scraped farther open.

"Nancy!" George hissed. "Get back here!" She beckoned from the side of the building. I scrambled to join her, squeezed up right against the wall.

I made it just as a large bald head came poking out the window, surveying the grounds. George and I held our breath as he turned his head side to side, looking for anyone on the run. If he looked directly below him, he would see George and me covered with dirt, breathing heavily. There would be no doubt that we were the culprits. I wasn't sure what the consequences of our actions would be, but I had a feeling they wouldn't be good. Not to mention that I wouldn't be able to solve the case.

The man looked left and right again. My leg was starting to cramp, and I could feel a cough tickling in my chest. I cast my eyes upward. I could see the bottom of the man's chin, where he had missed a spot shaving. All of a sudden a large drop of sweat came cascading through the air, landing right on my forehead. I bit down hard on my lip to stop myself from crying out.

Finally the man pulled back inside the room.

"I don't see anything. You sure you didn't just forget to close out the monitors?"

"I guess, maybe," the other guy said dubiously.

We heard the window slide shut. George and I took that as our cue and sprinted around the corner back toward the lobby.

Once we were safely back inside, blending in with the guests, we slowed down to a walk.

"That was close!" George exclaimed.

"Really close!" I agreed. "The worst part is we're no closer to figuring out what happened! For every piece of evidence we have that says it's Tami, we get another pointing toward Joe."

"You don't think they're working together, do you?" George asked.

"I guess it's possible, but it seems unlikely."

Before I could elaborate, George's phone started buzzing and buzzing and buzzing.

"What's going on?" I asked.

George slowly turned her phone to me. "I set my phone to notify me when people tweeted about Brady."

"What's going on?" I asked.

"Apparently Brady just tweeted that protesters are trash and deserved to be trashed like his room was. People are not happy with him. They're saying this is just more evidence that he incites violence against people who disagree with him. It's already been retweeted over eight hundred times, and more and more people are saying that they're going to protest his show."

"Why would he tweet something like that? He knows people would get mad."

George shrugged. "Did you consider that maybe he's doing this to himself? Maybe he doesn't want to do this tour. I read that he stopped touring for a year because he got hit with stage fright. Maybe that video going viral made it start to come back and he wants out."

"I don't know. This seems like a lot of trouble to get out of his tour."

"He'd probably face a lot of fees from the venues if he just canceled. If he argued that his safety was at risk, then he could probably get out of the performances without paying anything."

"Maybe. We need to talk to him and get him to tell us why he sent that tweet."

George and I headed back up to Brady's room and knocked on the door. Bess answered.

"Oh my gosh. You two are filthy! What happened?"

"It's a long story," I answered.

"Well, come on. We need to get you cleaned up."

We went into the room, but Bess veered off into the bathroom. Ned and Brady were hunched over the table, working on piecing together another page from the notebook.

"Whoa, Nancy," Ned said. "Did you dive into a pile of dirt?"

"Basically," I said.

"That's my girl." He winked.

Bess came back from the bathroom armed with two wet washcloths.

"Start scrubbing," she said, hovering over us. Sometimes George teased Bess that she was the den mother of our group. Bess found it annoying, but I had to admit George wasn't wrong.

I ran the washcloth over my arms. The small white piece of terry cloth quickly turned a light brown.

"Why'd you send that tweet?" George asked Brady without any warning. I probably would have tried to be a little gentler in my approach, but George was always the most direct of my friends.

"Because I'm trying to believe that your friend

Nancy is going to save my show and I wanted people to come to it?" Brady said, sounding confused.

"And you thought threatening protesters was a good way to do that?" George continued.

Brady looked at her like she was crazy. He pulled out his phone. "Um, I don't think saying 'Can't wait to do a show in my old college stomping grounds, River Heights! Hope to see you there!' really qualifies as threatening," he said, reading from his phone.

"No, the other tweet," George said.

"That's the only tweet I've sent all day," Brady said.

"I was right next to him, looking over his shoulder, when he tweeted," Ned said. "That's what he said."

Brady held out his phone and I could see it. Sure enough, the tweet said exactly what he had just read.

"George, let me see your phone." She handed it over. It was still buzzing incessantly as people retweeted the incendiary tweet over and over. It was up to three thousand retweets just in the past ten minutes. I looked between the account on Brady's phone and the one on George's. They had the same profile picture and the same bio, but there was one difference.

"This account's username is @Brady0wens with a zero, not with the letter *O*," I exclaimed. "This is a fake."

"Ugh," Brady groaned. "Whoever runs that account has been a pain in my neck for the past several weeks. Everyone thinks it's me, and its mission in life seems to be to get people mad at me. It tweets terrible, terrible things. I thought about complaining to the company. But if they consider it a parody account, it's protected as free speech, and they won't do anything to shut it down."

"Besides," said Bess, "wouldn't that be a little hypocritical if you tried to restrict someone else's free speech?"

"It's different," Brady protested.

"How?" Bess asked. I was curious myself. It didn't seem like it was different, and I thought she had a good point. I was a little surprised that Bess was speaking up. She usually avoids conflict, but she must really feel that Brady was in the wrong about his mugging joke.

"It's different," Brady explained, "because when I make offensive comments, I own them. I don't try to trick people into thinking someone else said them. This person is trying to make people hate me."

I could see Bess taking a deep breath to respond—because she's so kind, people think Bess is meek, but she is a bulldog when she feels passionately about something—but I needed to jump in. This was the type of question that could be debated for hours in a class like Professor Vega's, and it wasn't going to help me solve this case.

"Let's refocus," I said. "This tweet is very specific. They seem to know that your room was trashed. Have you said anything publicly about what happened?"

"No, of course not!" Brady said. "It's humiliating. Why would I tell anyone?"

"So," I said, feeling the excitement build in my chest and spread through my body the way it always did when I finally had a break in a case, "that means the culprit must have tweeted this." I turned to George. "Is there a way to track who the owner of this account is?"

"Sorry, Nancy," George said. "Even if I could, it would take several hours. Way more time than we have."

"Okay," I said. I knew this was key and I was going to figure out a way to capitalize on it. "We'll just have to do this the old-fashioned way. We have two prime suspects, Tami and Joe," I said.

"Are you still carrying on about Joe?" Brady asked. "Because this proves it's not him."

"How so?" I asked.

"Because Joe's an old fuddy-duddy," Brady said. "He still owns a record player. He reads books on paper, not on an e-reader. I'm pretty sure he still uses a typewriter."

I remembered the typewriter I had heard Joe using in his office and realized Brady was right.

"So you're saying Joe wouldn't know how to set up a fake Twitter account?" I asked.

"I'm saying he doesn't know what a Twitter account is," Brady said.

"So it's gotta be Tami," said Ned.

"Yeah," I said, feeling a grin spread over my face. This case was so close to being solved. "Now we just need to prove it!"

CHAPTER NINE

Switcheroo

"WE NEED TO FIND TAMI," I SAID.

"She just posted a photo from Joe's office," George said, looking at her phone. "I think she's still there."

"Let's go!" I said.

Ned, George, Bess, and I all headed out.

"Save my show, Nancy Drew! You're my only hope," Brady called after us.

We raced back across to the Arts Complex. "I'm definitely getting my workout in today going back and forth between the hotel and the Arts Complex," George commented.

"It does feel like we've been on a loop," I agreed, as we headed back up the stairs to Joe's office.

We entered the office again. It was still full. If anything, there were more people here. I spotted Tami standing in the corner. She had her phone out and was staring at it avidly.

"George, does she have the same phone as you?"

George peered over. "Looks like it."

"Great, can I borrow yours?"

George looked at me. "It's not that I don't want to do anything you need to help solve this case. I always have your back, but . . . you know this phone is my baby. It's my life. My best friend."

"Hey!" Bess cried.

"My best nonhuman friend," George clarified, but Bess continued to glare at her, unconvinced.

"I promise you will get it back safe and sound," I assured her.

George kissed her phone. "Goodbye, my precious. You'll be okay, don't worry."

She handed over the phone.

I turned toward Tami, plotting my move. I would have only one shot at this.

"I feel naked," George muttered behind me. "It just feels wrong not to have Chester."

"Chester?" Ned asked.

"I named my phone Chester," George stated, as if that was the most normal thing in the world. I wasn't looking, but I knew Ned was shaking his head, bemused.

"Here, hold mine," I said, handing her my phone.

"Tami! Check this out!" a woman to Tami's right called out. Tami pivoted. Her phone was still in her hand, but she was no longer paying attention to it. It was time to make my move.

"Bess, your purse!" I hissed.

Bess didn't hesitate. She handed her purse over, and I slung it over my shoulder, pleased by its weight. She carried giant purses, which magically always seemed to have anything we needed in them. "When I'm within a foot of her, call out my name," I whispered. My friends nodded, their faces set.

I took a deep breath and marched toward Tami.

I got closer and closer, until I was only a few inches away. Then, right on cue, I heard Ned call out, "Nancy!"

I spun, twisting my torso with vigor, allowing the centrifugal force on Bess's purse to make it spin out. It whacked Tami right across the arm. It wasn't hard enough to hurt, but it definitely surprised her. Her phone was flying out of her hand and scattering across the floor. The contents of Bess's purse also went everywhere. I still cradled George's phone in my left hand. The whole room turned to look at me.

"I am so sorry!" I exclaimed.

Tami looked at me. Her mouth gaped open.

"Watch where you're going," she finally snapped.

"I am so sorry," I repeated. "Let me clean this up." Crouching down, my hands moving quickly and in all directions, I began picking up the contents of Bess's purse: Kleenex, lip gloss, breath mints. I glanced up and saw that Tami was watching my hands fly over the mess, her eyes bouncing back and forth.

"I can't believe how careless I was. I'm not used to carrying this purse," I prattled on, wildly gesturing with my right hand and using a trick I had learned from a pickpocket I caught a few years ago. Distract with one hand; pick up with the other. With my left hand, I dropped George's phone and palmed Tami's, quickly depositing Tami's phone into Bess's purse.

I picked up the phone on the ground, which was George's, and held it out toward Tami.

"Here's your phone," I said with an apologetic smile. "Again, I am so sorry!" I said.

"Yeah, fine," Tami grumbled.

I scurried back to my friends and handed Tami's phone to George.

"Quick," I said. "We only have a few minutes before Tami realizes we switched phones."

George grabbed the phone and started working her magic.

"I'm glad you put a phone in her hand," Ned whispered. "She was starting to get jittery."

All of a sudden, out of the corner of my eye, I saw

Tami marching toward us. One glance back at George told me she was still working.

"Excuse me," Tami said curtly. "You took my phone."

"What's that in your hand?" I asked, as innocent-sounding as I could. Behind me, I felt Ned and Bess slide in front of George, blocking Tami's view of her.

"I'm assuming it's yours," Tami said, as if I was the dumbest person in the world.

"Oh, did I switch them?" I asked.

"I guess so," Tami said.

"Sorry about that!" I said, digging in my purse. I threw a quick look behind me. Bess subtly moved her fingers in a circular motion, telling me to stretch it out with Tami to give George more time.

"Let me see if I can find it in here," I said. "Hang on one second."

Tami sighed and actually tapped her foot. I had always thought that was just an expression. I had never seen anyone do it.

"You know," I said, deciding to take advantage of

our situation, "I noticed earlier that members of your group were spreading that tweet about Brady saying that protester should be trashed."

"Yeah, of course," Tami answered. "People need to see what lines that man is willing to cross."

"Well, I don't know if you knew this, but Brady didn't actually tweet that," I said as I continued pretending to search Bess's purse, again using my fake-innocent voice. I was curious to see how she would react.

"Yeah," Ned chimed in. "That's actually a fake account."

Tami stared at us. "What do you mean?"

Ned and I showed her the fake account name. I pointed out the zero in his Twitter handle.

Tami sighed, "Well, I didn't know. I'll tell the group."

"But you know," Tami went on, "Brady *could* have tweeted that trash tweet. The fact that I couldn't tell means that what he does post is over the line."

She didn't let me respond. "Can I just get my phone back, please?" She held out her hand.

I resumed digging in the purse. "Oh, sure. Sorry," I said.

I felt Bess nudge me. I slipped my right hand back and Bess dropped the phone into it. I palmed the phone, reached that hand into the purse, and then pulled it out, extending her phone toward her.

"Thanks," she said, handing George's phone back to me and turning away.

As soon as she turned, Bess, Ned, and I all pivoted toward George. Her face was downcast and she shook her head.

"I didn't find anything that indicated she's behind that account," she said.

"She wasn't acting like she controlled it either," I said, ushering everyone out of Joe's office and into the hallway, so we could talk more freely.

"It's possible she hid it really well, but I checked all the obvious places," George said. "She seems to have only one account."

I had been so sure that Tami was our culprit. The case had felt so close to being solved just a few minutes ago, and now it felt further away than ever. I had no more suspects.

"I'm sorry, Nancy," George said. "Maybe if I'd had more time, I could have found something."

"It's not your fault," I said. "We just need a new angle."

"Let's go outside," Ned suggested. "Fresh air always helps me think."

But as soon as we pushed open the door, we found ourselves in a huge mob. There were hundreds of people everywhere, streaming toward the theater.

Some were holding signs that said TRASH BRADY OWENS! Others were chanting, "Stop Brady! Stop Brady!"

"Holy cow!" Bess exclaimed.

"I can't believe how big this got," I said.

"That's the power of social media," said George. "The idea of protesting in front of the theater just went viral."

"It sure did. It looks like people from all over town are here," Bess said.

"Yeah, I see a lot of people I recognize from school here," Ned added.

"You were right, George," I said, "when you told those women that people are always watching online. I guess they just needed a little push to get them to take action in real life."

"How does Brady perform in an environment like this?" George asked.

"Nancy!" I heard behind me, barely rising over the noise of all the protesters. I turned to see Joe Archer fighting through the crowd.

"Did you figure out who's behind this yet?" he asked.

I shook my head.

"It's five o'clock, Nancy. If I don't have a culprit in an hour . . ." He trailed off.

"I know. I'm working as fast as I can."

"Well, either way, I have to put more security out here now. This crowd is out of control," Joe said. He paused for a moment. "It's really terrible timing, too. We're getting the Dutch masters show ready tonight, but I don't have a choice. We have to put all our security on this madhouse." He indicated the mass of people in front of us.

"Does that mean *The Zebra Finch* is coming tonight?" Bess said.

Joe nodded miserably. "Before Brady became a lightning rod for controversy, it would have been fine. We had plenty of security to cover both events, but now . . ."

"Don't you think you should delay moving in *The Zebra Finch*, then?" asked Bess.

"Do you know how many months of negotiations it took to get Donna Ellis to let us exhibit that painting? She is a nervous mess about letting this painting out of her vault. If I ask to change one detail, the whole arrangement will fall apart and I'll have to explain why one of the first performing arts shows was protested and the most famous painting in our first visual arts show was pulled. The Arts Complex would officially be a failure. It would take years to recover from that reputation. Who would risk spending the money to travel here if our shows fall apart at a moment's notice?"

We stood in silence for a moment, all lost in our own thoughts. The Arts Complex was great. The space was amazing, and Joe seemed like he had really interesting ideas for it. I didn't want it to fail. I thought about how much money the Towering Heights Resort had put into their renovations. If the Arts Complex didn't draw the crowds they expected, they would lose money, and a lot of people like Pete—and even the security guards after George and me—would be out of jobs. I couldn't let that happen.

I smiled confidently back at him. "I'm going to figure out what's going on here," I told Joe.

CHAPTER TEN

A Mysterious Man

"I HOPE SO," JOE SAID. "IF WE DON'T KNOW who the culprit is in an hour, I'm going to have to cancel the show altogether. I can't risk anyone getting hurt."

Joe walked away and I turned to my friends. "Let's go someplace quieter," I said.

A few minutes later we were sitting in the Coffee Cabin, sipping iced teas. It was technically closed, but George had a set of keys and her boss didn't mind if we came after hours as long as we paid for our drinks and left everything exactly as we had found it. It was a huge perk of George working there. We considered it our unofficial clubhouse.

"We need to go back to basics," I said. "I feel like we're not approaching this case from the right direction. The biggest problem in my mind is that we don't know the motive. Is this culprit trying to get Brady's show canceled? Are they trying to destroy Brady's career?"

"How do we figure that out?" Bess asked.

I took a long sip of my iced tea. "I don't know," I sighed. "But I think the tweet is key. It kicked this whole situation into another gear. But if it's not Joe and it's not Tami—and I think we have pretty good evidence that it's not either of them—how do we figure out who it is?"

"I have an idea," George said.

We all turned to look at her.

"Have you guys ever heard of something called social engineering?" she asked.

Neither of us had.

"Well, social engineering is when instead of using

computer programs to hack into someone's account, people use their knowledge about that person to guess their password."

"What do you mean?" asked Ned. I was glad he asked, because I wasn't sure I was following.

"Well, a famous example is a few years ago, when a man in Florida broke into the e-mail accounts of a lot of celebrities, but he wasn't a computer programmer or anything. He was just a really big fan. He read everything he could about the various famous people and learned everything he could—what street they grew up on, their pets' names, and so forth—and used that to guess their passwords. He got into the private e-mails of about twenty movie stars. He tried to argue that he hadn't done anything wrong. He claimed what he did wasn't actually hacking, since he'd used only public information."

"Well, that's ridiculous," Bess said. "That's like when Jessie at summer camp tried to argue that she hadn't done anything wrong reading my diary because it didn't have a lock on it."

"I agree," George said. "And so did the courts. He's in prison now."

"So what are you saying?" I asked. "That we should social engineer the Twitter account?"

"Yeah, but like reverse social engineer it," George said. "Even though this person is tweeting in the voice of Brady, they can't help but let aspects of themselves through. If we read the tweets, we can pick out information about the culprit and start to paint a portrait of him or her."

"George, you're a genius!" I exclaimed.

George blushed and shook her head. She always gets really squirmy if you try to give her a compliment.

"It says here that the Brady Owens—with a zero—account has made four hundred tweets," Ned said.

"So what if we each take a hundred tweets?" I said. Everyone nodded. "Let's go clockwise, so George, you take the first hundred, Bess the second, Ned the third, and I'll take the last."

"I'm glad tweets are only a hundred forty characters!" Bess said.

"Me too," I agreed. "We only have forty-five minutes to do this! Start reading!"

We all went quiet and bent over our phones. If anyone looked at us through the window, they would think we couldn't stand talking to one another, as we all ignored the others and stared at our phones. I quickly scrolled to the bottom of the fake Brady's account and started reading.

It was exhausting reading tweet after tweet from this account. They were all so angry. Most of them just felt whiny, like the whole world was out to get the operator of the account. *Explaining how to use the remote to my grandma for the hundredth time*, one tweet read. "Feel like I'm stuck in Titian's painting of Sisyphus." I didn't know the painting, but I did know that Sisyphus was a character from Greek mythology who is punished in the underworld by having to push a boulder up a hill over and over again, unable to actually complete the task.

"Hey," Ned asked. "What day was the water main break on Maple that caused that flooding?"

"Oh," Bess said. "Wasn't that in early April?"

"Yeah, April twelfth," George confirmed after a quick search online.

"Well, on April twelfth, this account tweeted that their street was flooded. 'Beginning to look like Claude Monet's *Flood Waters* here,'" Ned read, before looking up, excitement flashing behind his eyes. "I think that proves that the culprit lives in River Heights. This isn't someone who came from out of town."

"Wait," George said. "Claude Monet's a painter, right?"

"Ya," I said. "A French impressionist."

"Because I saw some tweets in my batch that talked about art too. Actually, one mentioned *The Zebra Finch*," she said, "which is kind of a weird coincidence. Here, let me find it. 'Waiting for the cable guy to come and fix my TV. Said they'd be here by twelve thirty. Two o'clock still not here. Feel like the Zebra Finch, chained to my perch.'"

"Mentioned art in a bunch of mine, too," Bess chimed in.

"Mine too," I said.

"So our culprit lives in River Heights and is into art," George said.

"More specifically, I think they're into painting," I said. "Did you see any mentions of sculptures or photographs in your tweets?"

Everyone shook their heads. "I think we need to go back to Erica Vega," I said. "It feels too coincidental that the protests are being led by people who met in an art class and our culprit is passionate about painting. I think she knows more than she's letting on."

"Let's go!" Ned said. "We have twenty-eight minutes!"

We quickly threw out our iced-tea cups, put the pad of paper back in the storage room, and placed the chairs on top of the table. The Coffee Cabin looked like we had never been there.

We headed back to the Arts Complex.

"Maybe we really got this case wrong," I said. "Maybe Brady's not the target at all. Maybe this is about revenge against the Arts Complex. Do you remember any stories about people not liking the complex or being mad that Joe Archer was hired to run it? Maybe someone wants it to fail."

Bess, Ned, and George all shook their heads. "After the controversy over the design worked itself out, I thought everyone felt pretty positive toward it," Ned said.

"Yeah," George agreed. "All the blogs and everything I read thought Joe was a great hire."

"Well, it doesn't mean that someone didn't feel slighted," I said. "The board couldn't know that Joe would want to leave his job in San Francisco and come back to River Heights. They must have interviewed other people."

"That's another thing to ask Erica," Bess said.

We rounded the corner to the street the Arts Complex was on. Outside the theater, it was still jam-packed with protesters, but Joe's extra security guards had moved everyone onto the sidewalk, so they were no longer blocking the street. All in all, it did seem more orderly. I knew that Brady was disappointed, but there was no doubt that Joe had made the right decision in assigning more security to the protest.

Fortunately for us, the back entrance that was closer to the visual arts side was clear. In the loading dock sat an unmarked van.

Bess hit me on the arm. "Do you think *The Zebra Finch* is in there?"

"Oh, maybe," I said.

Bess looked like a girl staring at the boy she had a crush on. Her eyes were wide, her mouth slightly agape.

"You can stare as hard as you want, but you're not going to be able to see it through the sides of the van," George pointed out.

"I know, but just to know it's so close . . . I can't describe it. It's like if you knew Sherlock Holmes was in that van, Nancy."

"Sherlock Holmes is fictional," George pointed out.

Bess sighed, frustrated.

I pulled on the complex's back door and was surprised to find it open.

"That's weird," said George. "I thought we'd have to work a lot harder to get in."

"Me too," I said.

"Guess we're finally getting a lucky break," Ned said.

We headed down the hall to Erica's office. George had looked up where it was before we left the Coffee Cabin. As we turned a corner, I spotted a man walking in front of us. He was sporting a suit and a baseball cap.

"Hey," I whispered to George. "Doesn't that look like that man on the surveillance footage who was avoiding the cameras?"

George nodded. "Same build, same outfit."

"Look at his sleeves," Bess hissed. I didn't know what she meant at first. He was a good twenty feet in front of us and his arms were swinging as he walked, but suddenly it clicked.

"Gold buttons!" I said.

"Do they have anchors on them?" Ned asked.

"Only one way to find out," I said as I picked up my pace to catch up with the man.

"Excuse me," I called out. He didn't turn around.

I walked even faster and called out again, more loudly. "Excuse me!"

The man stopped and turned around. He had slight features and pale skin and wore glasses, but I barely looked at his face. My eyes went straight to his jacket. There, right in the middle between two other buttons, was an empty space.

"Yes?" he said.

"I think you lost a button," I said, reaching into my pocket and pulling out the button we had found in Brady's room.

I didn't think it was possible, but his face went even paler and his eyes wider. I don't know if it was the look on my face or that he knew where he had lost it, but after a second's hesitation, he turned and ran.

I didn't think; I just ran after him.

"Nancy! Wait!" I heard Ned call from behind me, but I had worked too hard and we were too close for me to wait.

I followed the man as he ran down the hall and through a door, which led to a flight of stairs. I sprinted down. The pale man was surprisingly fast, and I wasn't gaining any ground on him. I could hear his footsteps echoing ahead of me. Behind me I could hear my friends hurrying to catch up.

We went down three flights of stairs until I watched another door open. I ran after him to find myself in a huge open space. It looked like it was the storage area; there were leftover construction materials, racks full of costumes for future performances, teaching supplies, and items I couldn't identity covered in tarps.

I stood in the doorway and listened, but all I could hear was my own labored breathing as I struggled to catch my breath from my sprint.

I saw a flash of movement to my right and headed in that direction, picking my way through the jumbled maze. I couldn't imagine where all this stuff had come from. The Arts Complex had only been open for a few months.

Suddenly there was a noise behind me, but before I could pivot to see what it was, something smashed into the back of my head and the world went black.

CHAPTER ELEVEN

Confession

I FELT LIKE I WAS ON A BOAT BEING ROCKED back and forth.

"Nancy! Nancy!" I heard vaguely, as if someone was saying my name far away, through a bank of fog, making the noise muffled. I was aware of a throbbing pain in the back of my head.

"Nancy, Nancy!" I heard again, and the world sprang into focus. I saw Ned's face hovering above mine, his expression worried.

"Thank goodness you're awake," he said, smoothing my hair back from my forehead gently.

My surroundings were strange and I struggled to remember where I was. Suddenly it all came rushing back to me and I sat bolt upright.

"We have to catch that man!" I said, frantically trying to get to my feet, but as I rushed to stand, the world started to spin, and I felt my stomach turn. I sat back down with a *thud*, cradling my head.

"Hey, take it easy," Ned said. "We caught him."

"What?" I asked, quickly looking from the floor to his face and regretting it immediately.

"He's right over there," Ned said. He moved a little to his left, where I saw the man sitting calmly in a chair. George and Bess were standing on either side of him, guarding him. He didn't seem like he was trying to get anywhere, though. If anything, he seemed relieved to be sitting in the chair.

"What happened?" I asked. "How did you catch him? Did he confess?"

Ned laughed. "Slow down. I can only answer one question at a time."

"Sorry," I said. "First tell me what happened."

"George figured he wouldn't lead you into the basement if there wasn't an exit down here, so she recorded some audio of us talking and came in here playing that, so he thought all of us were here. Meanwhile Bess and I ran as fast as we could to the other side of the building. We found the exit and waited for him. He walked right into us."

"Literally," Bess said.

"Here, listen," George said. She held up her phone and I heard George say, "Through here," followed by Ned saying, "Do you see Nancy?" And Bess, "I don't like this. I think we should call the police." Then "We can't leave Nancy alone!" Ned reprimanded her.

I laughed. "That's really great," I said. It was a pretty ingenious plan, too, especially since they'd had to come up with it on the fly.

"I'm just sorry we didn't get here before he gave you that nasty crack on the head," Ned said.

I shrugged. "It's a risk of the job," I said.

"Only when you go charging after someone without waiting for your backup," Bess scolded me.

I blushed. "You're right. I should have waited. I was just so excited to solve this case."

"It's not the first time; it won't be the last," Bess said knowingly.

I was so lucky to have friends who would go to such lengths to help me. I felt guilty that I had taken off without them. I wanted to say that it wouldn't happen again, but I knew that Bess was right. I would do it again. When I got hold of a clue, it was almost like I was possessed. I had to follow it, even if that meant getting into dangerous situations.

I took a deep breath. I needed to focus on this case. I looked over at the man. His facial expression hadn't changed once. It was completely impassive.

"Did he confess?" I asked Ned.

"We wanted to make sure you were okay before we talked to him. Besides, we thought the honor should be yours."

I nodded, wincing in pain.

"Can you help me up?"

Ned put his hands under my shoulders and helped

me to my feet. The world spun again, but after a few seconds it stilled. Slowly, Ned keeping his arm around my shoulder, we walked in front of the man.

"Let's start with your name."

The man checked his watch before answering. "My name is Louis Flynn," he said calmly. "And I am the man you are looking for."

"How do you know?" I asked.

"You're the teenagers trying to figure out who is harassing Brady Owens, right?"

"How do you know that?"

Louis shrugged. "Just from around town, I guess."

I exchanged looks with my friends. I had only been working on this case for half a day, and the whole reason I had been brought on was to keep it low profile. It seemed odd that he would have heard of us. "What exactly did you do?" I asked.

"I broke into Brady Owens's hotel room and trashed it. I also run a fake Twitter account that stoked people's anger toward Brady. My sister was mugged and she ended up in the hospital. What Brady said made me furious," he said calmly.

"What about Brady's notebook? Did you destroy that?"

Louis hesitated for a second before nodding. "I guess?"

"You don't remember?" I asked.

"I destroyed the room. If there was a notebook in there, it's possible that got destroyed too."

This seemed odd to me. Each page had been ripped into dozens of pieces. It didn't seem like something someone had done casually and wouldn't remember. It had seemed deliberate. I was formulating my next question when Louis reached into his pocket and pulled out his phone.

He looked toward George. "I deduce that you are the techie of this crime-stopping group." I could almost feel the hackles go up on the back of George's neck. He sounded condescending, like he was making fun of us for investigating this case.

Louis offered the phone to George. "You'll find proof that I ran the Twitter account here."

George looked at me before taking the phone, as if asking for permission. She could sense something was off too. It felt like a trap, but the back of my head ached and I still felt foggy, like I was processing the world 75 percent as fast as normal. I nodded toward George to take the phone. I didn't have any better ideas.

George flipped through the phone. Within a minute she was saying, "He's telling the truth. He does control the account."

We were all quiet for a moment. Then, "Well, I guess that's it," Ned said. "Case solved."

"Yeah . . . ," I said. And I guess it was. I had what I needed: a confession and proof. But it felt anticlimactic. Louis had confessed too easily, too calmly. In my experience, most culprits put up a fight to the very end or confess in a fit of righteous anger, justifying why they did what they did. No one had ever just stated it as if they were telling me what they'd had for lunch.

"Joe," Ned said on his phone. "It's Ned Nickerson. We have your culprit and proof, too."

Ned walked to another part of the storage area and I could no longer make out what he was saying. Suddenly the pain in my head became acute. I grimaced, and I must have looked bad because Bess came rushing to my side.

"We need to get you to a doctor."

"I'm okay. I just need some aspirin and maybe some ice," I said.

"Well, I can take care of one of those things," she said. She reached into her huge purse and pulled out aspirin and a bottle of water.

"I love your magical purse," I said.

Ned came back. "Joe will be here in a minute."

Sure enough, a minute later, Joe sauntered in, a security guard at his side.

"Louis? Really?"

Louis shrugged.

I handed Joe the phone, and George explained how Louis had sent inflammatory online posts to incite the protest against Brady's show tonight. "I can't believe this," Joe said. "He confessed?"

Louis just nodded his head and looked to the floor.

Joe sighed and rubbed his head, then turned to the security guard who had accompanied him. "All right, take him to the police station."

The security guard crossed to Louis, who put out his hands to be handcuffed.

"I can't believe I hired you to teach painting here after you told me that your work stopped selling and that you were desperate for a job. This is how you repay me?" Joe said, the anger finally pushing through his shock.

Louis kept quiet, and Joe shook his head in disgust.

After they left, Joe turned to me. "Good job, Nancy."

"So Brady's show, it's on?"

Joe nodded. "My security team is doing a great job keeping the crowd outside controlled, and now that you caught the culprit, I feel confident that there won't be any more hijinks during his set." He clapped his hands together. "As they say, the show must go on!"

Ned grinned broadly and put his hand on my shoulder.

"I need to go make sure everything is proceeding correctly, but thanks a lot, Nancy."

Joe left and Bess turned to me. "Are you sure you don't want to go to a doctor? We can take you right now."

"No," I said. "I want to see the show." Even though the case was solved, I couldn't shake the feeling that it wasn't over.

We exited the basement and headed back upstairs to the theater. We called Brady and he got us on the list to come in through the backstage area, so we could easily get in without having to weave through the crowds. I peeked through the window on the way to see the protesters below. The security team was there and the protesters were out of the street and were staying behind the barricades the guards had set up. They had plenty of room and no one was stopping them from holding signs or shouting slogans and they were not impeding people who wanted to attend the show. It seemed like everyone was getting along out there.

Brady greeted us, and he quickly thanked me, but I could tell he was distracted getting ready for his show and I didn't want to throw him off. This was a big night for him. We promised to catch up with him after the show and tell him everything that had gone on.

We were the first people in the theater. It was nice to sit in the quiet for a while, but I still felt on edge. I couldn't tell if it was just the leftover adrenaline from being attacked by Louis or something else.

"Everything okay, Nancy?" Bess asked.

"I don't know. I just feel weird," I said.

"You'll feel better once the show's over and you know the case is solved for good," Bess reassured me.

The theater started to fill up and there was a steady line of people streaming in. My dad came in, and we waved as he took a seat near the back. The protest had succeeded in getting a lot of people to show up outside the theater and yell, but it didn't seem like it had stopped anyone from actually attending. To my surprise, I saw Tami slide into the back. I gave her a little wave and she smiled back at me.

Soon the lights dimmed, and a spotlight on the stage came up, focusing on a plain wooden stool with a microphone in front of it in the center of the stage. A few seconds later Brady strode onto the stage. A feeling of electricity shot through the crowd. There were some cheers but also some boos. Brady didn't seem bothered. He just picked up the mic, moved the stand to the left of the stool, and sat down.

"Hello," he said. "How was your day? Me, personally, I've had better." There was a chuckle through the crowd, tentative; the audience seemed caught off guard by his casual opening. "Have you ever heard that phrase, 'there's no such thing as bad publicity'?" he asked. There was a louder chuckle. It was like a rising tide, as people allowed themselves to be amused. "I decided to test the limits of that phrase. I figured that the best way to start a tour is to make everyone hate you. It's a brand-new viral marketing technique. You should all try it.

"In all seriousness, I need to say something." He paused again. "I'm sorry. I should have said this two weeks ago when I encouraged that crowd to mug that heckler. It wasn't funny and I should have never said it. So I want to thank the River Heights Victims' Rights Advocates for organizing these protests these last couple of weeks. Their hard work has forced me to admit to myself and to you that I had made a mistake. I just wish I had realized it earlier. This is what happens when you procrastinate, kids: things get worse." The energy in the room shifted; the crowd was now fully on board with him. I looked over at Tami; even she was nodding in appreciation.

And then Brady jumped up off the stool. "And that's the last serious thing you're going to hear from me all night, folks. Who's ready for some jokes?" he said loudly.

The crowd cheered. Any trepidation they'd had was gone.

"As some of you may know, I went to college in River Heights." The crowd cheered. "I am so happy to be back and in this beautiful Arts Complex. My friend Joe Archer runs it, so when he called me and asked if

I would come perform here, I immediately said, 'How much are you paying me?' No, I'm kidding. Joe's a great guy. We were roommates in college. Do any of you have roommates?"

And with that he was off and running. He didn't tell jokes so much as tell stories that made you laugh. He may have felt like his notebook was essential, but to the audience, you'd never know he felt unprepared. He kept the audience laughing.

"See?" Ned whispered. "Everything's fine."

I was about to nod, when all of a sudden a fire alarm started blaring. "Fire! Fire!" a mechanized voice said. "Please exit the building! Fire! Fire!"

"Something is going on," I said as we stood up. Ned, Bess, and George all nodded. This was not a coincidence.

CHAPTER TWELVE

The Real McCoy

OUTSIDE, MY MIND WAS RACING. THE audience from the show was mingling with the protesters. No one knew what was happening. Joe and Brady stood off to the side. I caught Joe staring at me, disappointed. It felt like a punch to the stomach. I had let both of them down. I couldn't ignore the nagging feeling in my gut anymore.

"I think we got it wrong. I don't think Louis is the guy."

"He confessed. You saw his phone," Ned insisted.

"Yeah, but it was too easy. He was too calm. He

was motivated because of his sister, but he talked about what happened to her in broad generalities and was completely emotionless."

I turned to Bess and George. "You two have been by my side as I've caught dozens of culprits. How many have acted the way Louis did?"

My friends looked at each other. "None," they said in unison.

"But why would he lie?" Ned countered. "He went to the police station. He'll end up in jail."

"Will he? I don't think the Twitter account is illegal. He'll get in trouble for the room, of course, but with a good lawyer, all he'll end up doing is paying for the damages."

"Guys!" George exclaimed. "Louis is a pretty well-known painter. I just looked him up on Wikipedia. He's an only child. He did a whole series of paintings about the life of an only child. He was definitely lying about his sister being mugged."

We were silent for a moment as we processed what George had just told us.

"Okay," Ned conceded. "But why?"

"I think he was covering for someone. I think all this has been a distraction. The room was designed to scare Brady. The tweets were designed to get more people protesting. It feels like when a magician waves their right hand around so you don't pay attention to what their left hand is doing."

"Okay, so what is he distracting us from?" George asked.

That was the million-dollar question. Fire trucks pulled up and parked in the loading dock where the van had been parked. Maybe that van really was carrying *The Zebra Finch*. Suddenly incidents that had happened earlier started flashing in my head. It was like a montage in a movie: Joe telling me that because of the size of the protest, he was pulling security off the move-in of *The Zebra Finch*. The tweet that I now knew Louis had written that mentioned that same painting. The way Louis had kept looking at his watch as we had questioned him.

"Nancy, what is it?" Bess asked. My face must have given me away. "What did you figure out?"

"We need to get to the arts wing, right now!" I yelled. I didn't wait for them; I just started running. I got five steps before I remembered where this had gotten me the last time, and I slowed down long enough to let my friends catch up.

Together we rounded the corner to the arts wing. Inside an alarm was blaring, a different sound from the fire alarm.

"George, do you have your lock picks?" I asked.

"Do you even have to ask?" George responded.

She stepped in front of me, pulling a set of lock picks out of her pocket. Without hesitation, she brought two of the picks up to the lock, but when she went to put them in place, the door pushed open on its own.

"Of course," I said. "Erica already picked the locks for us!"

We rushed in and made our way to the gallery where the Dutch masters exhibit would open this weekend. The walls were lined with over twenty Dutch master paintings. There were stark portraits and perfectly crafted still lifes, but right in the middle of the east wall was a blank spot. We raced over. The name plaque was still there. It read THE ZEBRA FINCH.

"This whole case was just a distraction from stealing *The Zebra Finch*," I told them. "I knew I missed something!"

Bess let out an anguished cry. "I can't believe this," she wailed.

"The fire alarm must have covered the sound of the alarm when the painting was taken off the wall," George theorized.

"But even if the police didn't put him in jail overnight, there's no way Louis would have been processed at the station and gotten back here in time," Ned said.

I shook my head. "No, he must have an accomplice," I said.

"But who is it?" asked Bess.

Now that I understood what this case was about, all the pieces were snapping into place, and I knew the answer to that question. "Think about it," I said. "Who was the real brains behind the protests?"

"Erica Vega!" Ned, George, and Bess all said together. I nodded.

"Now we just need to find her . . . and *The Zebra Finch*," Bess said.

"Okay, but let's go in teams of two," Ned said. "No one gets bashed on the head again. We stick together."

We split up. Ned and I headed to the right, while George and Bess went to the left.

I looked down at the floor and something caught my eye. It looked like tracks in the wax coating of the floor.

"This way," I told Ned. "Follow these tracks!"

"How do you know this is her?" Ned said.

"She can't just waltz out with the painting under her arm. It's one of the most famous paintings in the world. She'd have to hide it somewhere, and it's like two and a half feet by three and a half feet. She can't just stick it in her purse."

"These are suitcase tracks!" Ned exclaimed.

"Exactly."

The tracks ended at a door marked EMPLOYEES

ONLY. I yanked it open. I was surprised to see a pair of legs kicking in my face.

"She's climbing out the window," I shouted.

Ned reached up and grabbed the legs, trying to pull Erica back down.

"Where's the painting?" Ned asked, as Erica thrashed her legs, trying to get free of his grip.

I looked around. There was no suitcase.

"She must have gotten it through the window first," I said. Bess and George came running up behind me.

"We'll go get it," Bess said.

They turned to head to the door, when all of a sudden the doors came flying open and police came running in.

"FREEZE!" they yelled. Instinctively we all put our hands in the air. Then suddenly one of them stopped. "Nancy Drew, is that you?" It was Officer Parker of the River Heights Police Department. "We're here responding to a burglary alarm. What are you doing here?"

Before I could answer, Ned yelled out, "She's getting away." He had let go of Erica's feet when the police came in, and fittingly, she had used the distraction to climb through the window.

"The thief just climbed through that window!" I told Officer Parker. "She has *The Zebra Finch*. You have to stop her."

Officer Parker hesitated for a second. All the other officers looked at him, waiting for directions. He was clearly torn between taking all of us in for questioning or listening to what I'd said. Finally he said, "If Nancy Drew says the thief is getting away, the thief is getting away. Let's go get her!"

They tore out of the gallery. My friends and I hesitated for all of two seconds before taking off after them.

We made it around the corner of the building to the parking lot just as Officer Parker was slapping handcuffs on Erica.

Another officer opened the suitcase a few feet away. He pivoted it toward us; there was *The Zebra Finch*, still in its frame, safe and sound.

Just at that moment, Joe came rushing over, followed directly by my father. They looked between my friends and me, Erica in her handcuffs, and the suitcase with *The Zebra Finch*. Joe stood there with his mouth opening and closing in shock as I could see him piecing together what had happened.

After a moment, Joe looked at Erica and asked, "Why?"

"I'm up to my eyeballs in student loans," she said. "I borrowed so much money to study art history in school and for what? To teach community art classes in River Heights?"

"This was just about money?" I asked. "Everything you taught about art and free speech and the responsibility of the artist was just to rile up protesters to provide a distraction for your heist? You didn't mean any of it?"

Erica gave me a withering look. "I meant every word. Two things can be true at once, you know. I can need money and I can believe that Brady Owens is an irresponsible artist and should be held accountable for his actions."

Joe grimaced. "I wish I had listened to what my community was trying to tell me," he told her. "This is supposed to be a space where River Heights can come together. I was so sure I was right, that I couldn't get in the way of free speech. But my community was trying to tell me something. They were trying really hard to get me to hear them. I should have listened. I should have met with them so we could come to a decision together. If I had, none of this would have happened."

Everyone paused to let his words sink in.

Officer Parker broke the silence, "Okay, it's time to go. Joe, we'll need you to come give a statement later on." He gave us a nod and lead Erica away.

Joe watched her leave, still processing everything that had happened. Then he turned to me. "Thanks for saving *The Zebra Finch*. I never could have lived with myself if it had gotten stolen on my watch."

"My pleasure," I said.

"I need to admit something else," he said. "I went up early to Brady's room and saw that it had been destroyed before I met him for lunch. My first thought was to run down to tell security. But then a little voice told me this break-in could be karma for what he'd done at that talent show so many years ago. I paced back and forth, wrestling with my conscience for what must have been fifteen or twenty minutes. I'm sorry to say, the little voice won in the end."

"I guess time doesn't heal all wounds," I said.

"I guess not," said Joe.

Suddenly the adrenaline that had been driving me for the past several hours drained out of me and I was exhausted.

"I think it's time to go home," I told them. "It's been a long day."

"Don't forget your injury," Ned reminded me.

"Injury?!" my dad squawked, approaching us.

"I just hit my head. I'm fine."

"It's more than that," Bess said. "She got hit hard."

"We're going to urgent care. Now," my dad said.

"What about the rest of Brady's show?" I asked. "You don't want to miss that."

"It's fine," said Ned. "We can say goodbye to him in the morning."

"Your head is more important than Brady's show," my dad barked. "Come on."

"Okay," I said. My head throbbed and I was starting to think going to see a doctor wasn't a bad idea.

The next morning Ned and I approached the Towering Heights Resort to find Brady packing up his car. The doctor had determined that I had avoided a concussion. She said to take it easy and rest, but I was lucky and had just ended up with a bad bruise.

"Heading to the next city?" Ned asked.

"Yep. Amherst, Massachusetts, here I come," said Brady.

"Sorry we missed the end of your show," I said.

"Are you kidding?" he asked. "As excuses go, 'I was saving a world-famous painting from being stolen' is one of the better ones."

I laughed.

"I just can't believe I was used as bait in an art heist. That's crazy stuff. Might be movie material, honestly."

I spotted Tami walking towards us, her arms

swinging in her signature confident stride. She walked right up to Brady.

"Hi, I'm Tami, I'm the leader of the River Heights Victims' Rights Advocates." She shook Brady's hand. "And I wanted to apologize."

"For organizing a boycott of my show?" Brady asked. "There's no need to apologize. I'm glad you did. You got me to listen to things I needed to hear."

"No, of course not. I'm proud of the work we've done. And I caught your show last night. I'm glad you apologized on stage; that was the right thing to do," Tami said. "I need to apologize about yesterday. You see, I went to your hotel room to deliver the signed petitions asking you to cancel your show, but when I got up there, the door was open. I saw your notebook just sitting on the desk and I could see that you were working on new jokes. And at that point you were still acting like jokes were just jokes. Like you could do anything without consequence. I thought ripping them up would finally get the message across. And I've felt badly about it ever since. Ripping up those pages goes against what I believe and it was wrong. I'm sorry."

Tami looked at Brady and waited for his response.

"You know what?" he said after a few seconds. "I'm glad you did it. You were right. Those jokes were destructive. They were so destructive that someone was able to use me and what I'd said to cause such a kerfuffle that she could try to steal a painting. If I wasn't a comedian who insulted people, she couldn't have used me. I need to start over and think about what I actually want to say, so I'm glad you came over and said sorry, but I am going to say thank you."

He reached out and shook Tami's hand again. Tami and Brady were smiling, both were clearly happy with the turn of events.

"All right, kids, I gotta hit the road if I'm going to make it to Amherst on time. Thanks for everything, Nancy. I hope Carson writes about this case in the Christmas letter. It's a doozy. Ned, good talking to you. Send me the link to the interview when it's up. Tami, thanks for hastening my artistic reinvention."

He waved goodbye and climbed into his car. He

honked his horn as he pulled onto the street, heading toward the highway. Tami took off back where she came from, but Ned and I stayed put for a moment.

"That was a close one," I said. "I almost didn't solve it."

"But in the end you did," Ned said. "You saved Brady's show and *The Zebra Finch*. Two cases in one!" He took my hand and squeezed it in congratulations. "What do you want to do today?"

"Want to edit the podcast and get it posted while the world is still talking about Brady Owens?" I asked.

"Sounds like a plan," Ned agreed, as we headed off to our day.